Published in 2013.

ISBN 978-1492285892
© 2013 Yvone Isaacs

Prepared for print by Callisto Green.

Leaving No Trace

Esther Peters

About The Author

A veteran nurse, **Yvone Isaacs** has spent the last two decades in pediatric nursing. The bulk of her experience is specifically in neonatal intensive care on three continents. Some of these nursing experiences are recorded in her first book, Seven Tiny Miracles. She has now turned her attention to writing medical mysteries. This is her first novel under the pen name Esther Peters. Visit her on the web at www.yvoneisaacs.com

Acknowledgments

I would like to express my appreciation to the many health colleagues who during the past twenty years have shared with me the secret lives of doctors outside the hospital buildings. I was also influenced by those colleagues who read my first book – which embraced the lives, loves and shortcomings of doctors – and who encouraged me to write more. Without their encouragement I would never have begun the journey. For all those 'silent' contributors who chose to remain anonymous, thank you – you know who you are.

Also, profound thanks to Vicki Watson, my editor, for her superb editing and her commitment to handling this project with just the right touch, and to Simon Ridge, for his excellent cover design and meticulous interior page layout. Kudos and gratitude to Anita Martin and Janet Henning, for their generosity of time and encouragement. You often believe in me more than I do myself. Thank you.

Dedicated to those readers who enjoy medical mysteries.

Thank you. You're appreciated.

The length of our life is less important than its depth.

− M. D. Fisher

Prologue

"This must look like an accident. Can you arrange that?" Thomas Valdane asked his companion. No one ever asked this question of a professional and Oliver Townsend could feel deep anger rising within him. No one ever insulted him and remained unharmed. He wasn't some amateur picked up from the streets.

He was tempted to reply with utter bitterness. Yes, I think I can manage that. Would you prefer an accident outdoors? I can arrange a plane crash, a traffic accident, or a disappearance in the French Alps? The French detective in Paris. Or he could get drunk and drown in his bath. The Turkish ambassador to New York. Would you prefer an accident indoors? I can arrange for him to break his neck falling down a flight of stairs. Or maybe he could fall asleep in bed with a lighted cigarette. But he said none of those things. Instead, he replied, "Sir, I can arrange an accident. No one will ever know."

He waited. Both men walked on the snow-covered park. The storm had passed, and had blown four inches of soft snow across the ground. Most of the trees lifted stark, bare limbs. But a few, such as the spruce and evergreen, kept their foliage, a green counterpart to the skeletal outlines of the other trees. The two individuals walked silently. Valdane

1

disliked having to avoid tripping on Townsend's Jack Russell terrier. The dog whimpered each time his paws sunk in the snow. Neither man appeared mindful of the dog's cries. It was not routine, yet not unusual either for owners to walk their dogs after a storm, even when the temperature was just eighteen degrees. So the two men would not attract any undue attention. Nobody would be likely to suspect that they were a professional killer and his employer.

Oliver Townsend was glad of this assignment. He was low on money and had demanded $75,000 to be paid in cash. An independent contractor, he'd discovered long ago that he had a talent not just for killing people. Anyone can buy a gun and shoot a relative or a friend. Oliver's talent was murdering strangers, leaving no evidence behind. His philosophy was to do his job and leave no trace. In fact, he possessed a strong moral code and would not work for drug networks. Not that they needed any assistance, being generally capable of killing anyone who hampered or bothered them in any way. He wasn't a sociopath or a serial killer either; Townsend thought the sheer ruthlessness and inhumanity of the drug lords was offensive and considered them off-limits. He had, on occasion, been hired by illegal networks in the United States, but they generally wanted another criminal killed and Townsend had no objection to taking such a job. They liked his style, for he killed without leaving a trace.

For a man in such a deadly business, he had a pleasant smile, a disarming manner and a vivacious personality. Strangers were charmed into perceiving him as a mild, pleasant little man, incapable of any violent act. While off-duty, he could be an amiable conversationalist. People meeting him thought his only flaw was that he talked too much.

His current employer, Thomas Valdane, looked young, possibly only in his late twenties had wide, blue eyes and brown sideburns down his angular jaw. Similarly, Oliver wore glasses but they had black rims and covered small, dark eyes. His hair was long and fell down below the collar of his jacket. Although walking slowly, he appeared agitated when alongside Townsend, who strolled through the snow as if he didn't have a care in the world. Both men were bundled up against the cold. Valdane knew his employee only by the name of Smith.

"The doctor is dead," Townsend said as they passed by a wooden picnic table.

"Yes, I caught a glimpse of the news before I left. It'll be a huge news story. May I ask how it was done?"

"He fell down the stairs. There shouldn't be any suspicions when the authorities investigate. The doctor lived in a large two-storey house. He slipped during the night and hit his head. Accidents happen, even to rich people."

Valdane looked pleased and excited.

"His death was necessary—"

Townsend waved his hand as if dismissing Valdane's words. He cared nothing about the rationalizations of his employers, all of which were lies anyway.

"I have no interest in your reasons for wanting the doctor dead, although from what I've read of his background, he was of considerably greater benefit to humanity than you will ever be. If his resume had been a bit more impressive,

I would have rejected the job. But others can carry on his work."

"The doctor was not as holy and honorable as some made him out to be," Valdane said, obviously stunned and upset by the killer's words. Valdane thought himself more enlightened and civilized than other men even if, now, he was a murderer. But what he had done, or at least put into motion, was necessary, he told himself.

"He had done much good in life and in death he did much good for me. Do you have the money?" Townsend asked.

Valdane nodded and passed a fat envelope to Townsend, who put it into his coat pocket. "You're not going to count it?"

"Of course not." Townsend smiled. "If the amount isn't accurate I'll come back and kill you."

The words were said in a mild tone but, even on the cold day, they sent a chill through the younger man. He coughed and spoke in a hurried tone. "In cash as you wanted. The remainder will be sent to the account you specified in three days. Seven days after that, you'll receive the final installment."

Townsend nodded. He had his own unique way of doing business. For the murder of Dr. Wesley Hunter, a very wealthy man, he had demanded $75,000. Some of the money was to be paid in cash and some sent to a special account he had set up for the purpose. When sent, he would transfer the money to several other accounts, and then close the original. It wasn't the perfect way to hide transfers, but the way he did it could confuse all but the shrewdest of fiscal examiners.

"Was it difficult?" Valdane asked.

"The act was not difficult. There was a good deal of planning and preparation. It was time-consuming but not unduly so. I expect the additional payments on time. Now we can go our separate ways."

"What if…if we need you again?" asked Valdane, his hands slightly shaking. He knew he could not disappoint his associate. His future depended on that.

"Then you will have to find somebody else."

Townsend wasn't surprised that Valdane used "we." He always knew the younger man was fronting for someone else. Townsend stopped and turned to look at Valdane. "The payment for this assignment was generous so I decided to do one job for you, but it ends there. I don't particularly like you, Mr. Valdane. And worse yet…" he pointed to his Jack Russell "Reggie doesn't like you. He usually likes everybody. That's a sign that I should not work with you again. You, and I assume the people around you, are nothing more than remorseless murderers. Good day."

Townsend walked on, leaving Valdane sputtering indignantly into the cold wind. The killer was suspicious about his employer. For a man, Valdane was a good makeup artist. Townsend was sure the sideburns and probably the hair were fake. Valdane had obviously been sent by someone. But that didn't matter. He hadn't told the younger man one thing. A smile played around the corners of the killer's mouth as he got into the car. Townsend was aware of

Valdane's aversion to the doctor. But he didn't need to know Valdane's intention, so as long as he received payment.

Chapter 1

Elm Grove, Nevada

The Previous Evening

It was six days before the Thanksgiving holiday. Dr. Wesley "Wes" Hunter had finished his online business meetings and was planning to join his wife at their villa in France within the next couple of days. He had done this in the last five years and it was practically the only time alone he had with his wife. Wes, as his friends called him, owned most of the real estate in Nevada. He owned four of the five golf courses in the region, two medical centers, banks, and the private airport. His oil fields extended beyond Nevada and his oil companies were mainly in the central and north-western states. Where he could, he had oil pipelined to other states in the east and southeast.

He had not slept in three days. The journey to and from Idaho where a gas fire almost destroyed three oil wells had sapped all his energy. He kept up his workout regime, as a retired surgeon should, but there were days when he wished he could take a vacation. Maggie, his wife, had left two days ago for France. Last night had been the first night back home, and sleep was elusive. He found himself dozing off and then waking him with a start – the patter of rain against the windows, the ticking of the clock or the rustle of the bedroom curtains when a gust of wind blew in. He had always been a light sleeper and tonight he seemed even less able than usual to settle down.

For a long time, Dr. Wes lay in bed dozing fitfully. After five hours of sleep he got up, troubled over his conversations with Ted Humphries, the manager of the Idaho company. He couldn't understand why someone would want to set fire to his oil fields – perhaps the company was being targeted by domestic terrorists. Accustomed as he was to his wife being away several times a year on vacation, tonight seemed different, and he wished that she was there beside him.

Between 6:15 and 7:30 every morning except on Sundays, before taking a shower, Wes would saunter down to the kitchen, make himself a pot of coffee and take a cup back with him to his office. He would check his appointments, open all the newspapers at the business section, and then settle back to read those he thought worth his time. The headline in last Thursday's Chronicle: 'URGENT Oil Meeting In New York' was still high on Wes's agenda. On Thursday evening just before settling for the night, Wes asked the housekeeper to prepare an early breakfast at 5 o'clock before his flight to New York.

Wes's preparation for Friday's meeting had been much anticipated and he knew that it meant bad news for his own domestic oil supply. After all, in the last three years, Wes had spent most of his time convincing the American government that there would be revenue for this country from his own supply. The alarm went off at 4:30 a.m. He felt very drowsy and could not lift his head fully, but when the aroma of fresh ham, eggs and pancakes filled the air, he reached over and pressed the intercom. "Mrs. Hinkley," he called. "I'll have breakfast in my study this morning."

"Yes, sir," replied Marian. She did not like to be called Mrs. Hinkley since her late husband was a wife-beater. How he died had never been made clear, but Marian had told the court that she'd found him in their bed with another woman and ran from the house. "That," she told the judge, "was the last time my son and I saw him." Five years ago, the Boston case had been closed due to lack of evidence.

Marian had been working for the Hunters for the past four and a half years now. She'd moved to Los Angeles after the trial and although she'd found housekeeping jobs in Hollywood, she'd never seemed to be happy with her employers. And then she'd an advertisement for a live-in housekeeper. Recognizing that it was near to where her son worked, she'd applied and moved to Elm Grove two weeks later. Her son, Steven Gifford, now in his mid forties, had worked for one of the doctor's oil companies in Utah as a production engineer. He'd been transferred to the central headquarters in Elm Grove to supervise the production of several regional oil fields, and to send weekly updates to Wes.

On the way to Wes's study that morning, Mrs. Hinkley found the doctor partway down the staircase, his head bloody. He was not moving. She immediately called the ambulance and started CPR. Dr. Wesley Hunter was transported to the emergency room at Elm Grove Medical Center. He was pronounced dead on arrival. The exact time of death would be determined by the County Medical examiner following an autopsy.

9

S andi Hunter Burnside, Dr. Wes's daughter, felt the chill of the autumn morning breeze the minute she got out of her car. Pulling her coat a little tighter around her shoulders, she ran across the parking garage, and took the elevator to her studio office at 3123 Sunset Plaza in Elm Grove. The air in Nevada at this time of year was much colder than where she'd lived in Los Angeles. Suddenly that particular set of feelings seemed like familiar ground. And then she remembered. Those were my best days with my father. She remembered how he'd always taken her skiing or watched her compete in some other winter activity. She glanced up at the sky. The crisp November day had turned into an overcast morning, the sign of an early winter.

Now an investigative reporter with Elm Grove station KLRU-TV, she knew most of the local police officers and all the investigators on the Elm Grove force. Sandi heard the ringing of the phone from her office as she opened the door. She was surprised but not alarmed when she picked up the receiver and heard the voice of Detective Allan Morrison. In a kind, yet saddened voice he told her that her father had just been taken to the medical center he had founded. The temperate words coming through the telephone receiver were like a knock-out blow to the head. Stunned, she fell back into her chair.

"Oh, no!" and then like a drowning person gasping for air, "How? When? Allan, what happened?"

"Preliminary indications are that he fell down the stairs at his home, Sandi. He was found by the housekeeper this morning. She phoned the EMTs, and then we were contacted. But your father was dead when the EMTs arrived. They couldn't revive him." He paused. "Sandi, we haven't released this information to the media yet, although I know you're obviously with the media yourself. But I thought you and your family would need some time. I'm so sorry. I can take you to the hospital. It'll only take us fifteen minutes to get there."

Sandi nodded absentmindedly. Right now, she was staggered by the news, unable to form a coherent sentence. She just muttered a vague affirmation into the phone.

Somewhere in the back of her mind, she knew the family – meaning her – would have to prepare a press release. Her father was a prominent figure not only here, but internationally as well.

Within seconds, Sandi knocked on her boss's open door and pushed it open. Before she had change to enter, Charlie Dunn came to meet her, placing his arm on her shoulders. He murmured, "Sandi, I'm so sorry to hear about your dad. He was a very kind man to our network."

"How did y...you know s...so soon?" asked Sandi, sobbing intermittently.

"There was breaking news on our sister station, KLTR-TV thirty seconds before you walked into my office. I'll have Tim, your favorite cameraman, drive you over to the hospital. I don't think you should go alone. And before you ask, take as much time as you need. We'll cover for you."

11

Sandi nodded and said swiftly, "Thanks for offering to drive me to the hospital, but Detective Morrison will be picking me up shortly."

"Call us if you need anything and the office will be at your disposal."

"Thank you, Charlie." Sandi returned to her office, gathered her purse and coat and locked the door behind her. Detective Morrison was due in five minutes.

For the first time in a long time, Sandi found it difficult to concentrate or process what had happened to her father. I'm too young to have lost both parents. I don't remember very much about my mom's death, only that it was a difficult time for Dad. How could he just die? My father was the healthiest man I knew for his age, she thought. Other things about her past came floating back as in a tidal wave. Maybe I shouldn't have left him for so many years. He was my only living parent. I must have been happy for fifteen years. How did it all come apart? Sandi wanted to forget the events of the last twenty years. I need to re-focus, she thought Take one day at a time.

Her thoughts were interrupted by Detective Morrison's arrival. She stepped into the police car, its lights flashing, and Allan was quick to recognize that his words would not console her. He drove Sandi through the familiar maze of traffic lights heading for Elm Grove Hospital. A thirty-minute drive took him only ten minutes, and he dropped Sandi in front of the emergency room's entrance. Those ten minutes seemed like an eternity as her other life with a police-husband-turned-private-investigator flashed in her memory. *Was the divorce only five years ago? And how hadn't I seen it coming? It was hardly credible that all those women had been related to work.* After the separation, Sandi had taken her father's advice and moved back to Nevada – her children were in college and no longer needed her close by. Her thoughts gathered momentum. *How can I carry on with both of my parents dead? I only came back to Elm Grove because Dad wanted me to. Okay, I've got to be brave – he would have wanted me to be brave and strong. I must. I must...for his sake and for my children's.*

As soon as the children had returned to college the following spring break, Sandi had left Los Angeles for Elm Grove. Her career as an investigative reporter for the sixty-two year old news director, Charlie Dunn of KRLU Channel 3 News had begun. That had been two years ago. Charlie had offered Sandi the job for the on-air six o'clock news team. He knew that with her legal training, she would be an asset at trials, and with her natural warmth, she reminded him of a young Farrah Fawcett.

The reporters surged in front of the emergency room. Sandi jumped out of the car trying to dodge a mob of reporters that continued to bar her way. The media tried to get comments from Sandi before she disappeared into the hospital. Raising and waving an arm, Sandi turned to the nearest. "As soon as we have any news, the family will make a statement. For now, we would ask that you kindly give us some privacy. Thank you."

Boston, Massachusetts

Dr. Wes's son, Bill, was the medical director of the pediatric department at Elm Grove Medical Center. He was heavily involved with the Board of Directors in all the hospitals that his father owned and made many deci-

13

sions on medical and health issues on behalf of his father, who became less accessible due to his oil businesses. There were often family clashes, as Bill and Dr. Wes could not agree on some of the health programs that needed Dr. Wes's input. Dr. Bill was a brilliant and successful pediatrician, an achievement Dr. Wes bragged about to his friends but never spoke about from father to son.

The hotel receptionist walked quickly to the lecture hall. Inside she could see a room filled with animated junior doctors at their first medical conference. She looked around the room to locate the main speaker – Dr. William Hunter. He was not hard to miss as he stood six feet tall among the others in the far corner of the room. Hurrying to his side, the receptionist said, "Dr. Hunter, there's a Detective Morrison on the phone for you, sir."

Bill walked to the adjacent hallway to take the call. After handing over to another colleague, he got on the first flight back to Nevada. He'd been married for ten years and had no children. When his wife left him a year ago, he buried himself deeply in his work but spent his weekends playing golf and his nights at the Le Paris Hotel and Casino. Bill and his dad had had many disagreeable words over the years, but Dr. Wes was always quick to point out that his son's work ethic was similar to his own father's – Patrick Hunter, who'd always been strong in his conviction and happy to work long and tirelessly to achieve his goal.

Seated on the plane, Bill recalled the last conversation he'd had with his father, who had chided him on his recent lifestyle, brought to his attention by older Board members. Bill had looked his father straight in the eyes and said, "I'm alone now, Dad. Since Karen left, my world has turned upside down. It's the only way I know how to ease the pain." Dr. Wes had looked at his son and said, "If you only knew…When I lost your mother to cancer, I was too overwhelmed with the loss and pain to really care for both of you. Sandi took a lot on her shoulders and helped me. I was so involved in the oil business that I somehow forgot how to be a father… One of these days, I'll…" My dad had never finished that sentence.

Paris, France

Eight hours later

To the media, Wes and Margaret Hunter appeared to have the perfect marriage. An attractive woman of Irish descent, Maggie hosted lavish business parties and entertained Wes's business friends and associates with total grace and aplomb. And when she wasn't doing that, she spent many mini-breaks in southern France at their villa, and devoted the rest of her time to promoting liberal causes. It was a perfect match. Everyone but Wes's children agreed.

Wes had been a widower for two years before marrying the ex-wife of New Jersey's Senator. The last couple of years had been difficult for their marriage, since Wes was spending more and more time with the geologists prospecting for new oil fields. His wife Maggie had been left alone a great deal.

Dr. Mathew Ross, the family's physician, was called in one evening to assist Mrs. Hunter in getting rid of a fever. "This is the first time my temperature has got up to 105 degrees," she explained. "Every time my husband leaves,

I seem to either have high fevers or pounding headaches. What can it be, Dr. Ross?" She eyed the doctor speculatively.

"Your husband is a very busy man, Mrs. Hunter. He was just like that in college – never rests until the job is done. He's a good man. We were best buddies then and now. Take these tablets every four hours and try to get some rest. I'll check on you in the morning."

Maggie noticed his hands as he checked beneath her jaw for any swelling or warmth. He was so gentle with her. Her eyes were glued to him. "What do your friends call you?"

"Matt. Or Dr. Matt."

"Well, Matt, I think you and I are going to become very good friends. We are going to forget all that doctor-patient relationship stuff."

"Friends?" If only she knew how much I've wanted her to say that…for many years. She should never have married Wes. Dr. Ross watched her closely. I can't resist this any longer. He said, "I'm already the family's physician."

"I know. I mean close friends."

Dr. Matt was not a man to go into anything haphazardly. But over the next two weeks, he made sure that he was always available when Maggie called for an appointment. Their little secret went on for the next few months. Since he frequented the house when Wes had his headaches, there was no way of avoiding her anyway. Matt couldn't think of one excuse to prevent himself going to bed with her. After all, he loved her.

"I'm leaving tomorrow for our Villa in France," Maggie said. "Wes and I are spending Thanksgiving over there this year. He's supposed to join me in five days. I don't want to be alone before he gets there."

Matt shook his head, but he felt the excitement building within him. The restaurant scene from the movie When Harry Met Sally flashed into his thoughts. His longing for Maggie prevailed above all the hurt and pain he knew Wes would feel when he found out about their affair. "Maggie, I …I can't leave now. I—"

As though reading his mind, Maggie laughed. "It'll be our little secret, won't it, darling?"

The affair lasted almost two years.

It was three-thirty in the afternoon in France. Maggie and Matt sat on the patio of her villa in the south of France sipping a Brandy Alexander. Maggie received the phone call from Detective Morrison and chartered a jet to fly her to the United States. At eleven o'clock in the evening, New York Time, Maggie boarded the Hunter's private jet for her flight to Nevada. It was a miserable twenty-four hours; she was afraid to close her eyes in case she missed another phone call.

Chapter 2

Summerlin County, Nevada

One Week Later

Few men in history have successfully navigated two careers in such starkly different professions as medicine and the oil industry, yet Dr. Hunter was known and respected in both. His death might have been noted, at least briefly, on the national news shows, but there were other, even more pressing events happening in the world on the day he died. The Middle East was imploding, federal authorities had just arrested three men accused of planning a terrorist bombing in Detroit, and the Commerce Department had released a report around the severe economic downturn. All took precedent over Dr. Hunter's death and the subsequent investigation.

Due to his wealth and fame, the funeral for Dr. Wes could have been a grandiose affair but that was not what the late physician wanted. In his will, he had made exact stipulations that he did not want a flowery and verbose sendoff. There would be a viewing of the body at the designated funeral home and then a quiet ceremony with family members and very close friends. The brief eulogy would be given by the Rev. Lawrence Savelle, a Methodist minister whom Dr. Wes had known for thirty years.

"Be brief, Larry," Dr. Wes had told the minister. "If I haven't made an impression on people in the sixty-plus years I have lived, perhaps a twenty-minute oration will impress them more." Reverend Savelle had laughed and assured Dr. Wes that his complimentary send-off would not be lengthy. So the funeral was held at the First United Methodist Church with a large crowd numbering more than two hundred family and friends.

Sandi and her brother, Bill, sat on the two front rows; Harry Burnside had joined his ex-wife and their two children, whilst Bill's wife had also joined him for the service. Dr. Matthew Ross sat next to Maggie Hunter. A bit too close, Sandi thought. He looked like he enjoyed comforting the widow. She pinched herself and shook her head. You shouldn't give credence to such thoughts on a day like today, she told herself. She knew about the close friendship between her stepmother – she abhorred that term – and Dr. Matt. She'd also heard the rumors that he'd been in love with Maggie long before she'd married Dr. Wes. Sandi shook her head again. This was not the time to think such thoughts.

She sighed as she watched Marian Hinkley enter the chapel. Marian had asked for permission to attend and, because she had been a loyal member of staff for years, the family allowed it. It must have been a shock for her finding the body and she'd been quite shaken when she relayed the story to police. Still, Sandi felt there was a coldness about the housekeeper. She had always been cordial and certainly did her work efficiently but there was a chilly aura around her. Perhaps Marian was an introvert and simply did not project warmth. But from time to time, Sandi thought there was a darkness beneath the efficient smile.

Sandi shook her head. After an unexpected death in a family, survivors can act and think in strange ways, she knew only too well. Stop it, she told herself. Most Hunter family members were charismatic. At parties they'd dance on tables and stay up until dawn. Marian Hinkley was not odd simply because she was more subdued than the Hunter family.

Two older men, Dr. Stewart Richardson and Eldon Lancer, walked in with their wives. The two had been friends with Dr. Wes since college. In fact, for twenty-five years, the three had played golf every year on Christmas Eve; it had become a ritual. Dr. Wes was often away on business in December, but he always flew back to play eighteen holes with Stewart and Eldon. Dr. Wes was a Type-A personality – dynamic and gregarious. As such, he was always competitive, even in a golf game. But Sandi knew that the one time his competitiveness lessened was the annual Christmas Eve golf game. Even if he lost, Dr. Wes was laughing and smiling as the trio walked to the clubhouse. He lived a high-tension life but Christmas Eve golf served as a natural tranquilizer, better for the soul than meditation for a Buddhist monk. The three men would go into the clubhouse, have a few drinks and swap tales, before returning home to their families.

Dr. Richardson was a research scientist at the genetic engineering facility. He dreamed of a future without cancer or diabetes. Such a future, once thought impossible, was now within humanity's grasp, he always said. Although not born in Britain, he had an English accent. Or at least speech that sounded like an English accent. Born with a congenital speech impediment, he'd worked with a series of speech therapists. They'd corrected the impediment but the result was this slight British accent in Richardson's speech, which the scientist didn't mind at all. In fact, it rather amused him.

Dr. Wes wasn't as 100 percent sold on the genetic future as his friend, but Dr. Wes did believe that genetic research could discover cures for many of the serious diseases plaguing humans.

Eldon Lancer had made his fortune in insurance, real estate and timber. Like Dr. Wes, his family had been relatively prosperous but he had doubled his fortune many times over. A likeable man with a quick smile and a ready laugh, he also had a keen business mind. He had made himself an expert on the stock market and had made several shrewd guesses on market investing that had always paid off. He also had an acute understanding of his own nature, something totally alien to most men. He'd married in his mid-twenties and the six-year marriage produced two sons, something he was happy about because he'd wanted heirs. But since the divorce, Lancer had focused on his business, although it was acknowledged he was a good – although often absent – father to his two sons, who were now vice-presidents in the same company.

Five other men and one woman were also seated in the pews. They were, Sandi knew, employees from her father's oil businesses. Although one of the headquarters for Hunter Oil was in Elm Grove, many of his colleagues were in the South Dakota offices of the firm. Steven Gifford represented the local office. She knew Dr. Wes had thought very highly of Gifford.

Sandi thought she recognized one of the men now siding into a pew, a stocky man with a ruddy face. She was sure she had met him at some time in the past but she couldn't remember his name. The others she didn't recognize. The woman was a tall redhead, beautifully dressed in a pale blue outfit, which suited her. She didn't seem to be attached to any of the men. There were rumors of some rancor in the executive offices and her father had briefly alluded to what he called 'minor disagreements' recently. But his tone had indicated that the disagreements were not minor at all. She shrugged. This was not the time to think about that either.

A trio of singers sang Amazing Grace, one of Dr. Wes's favorite hymns. When they left, Reverend Savelle stepped to the podium. He opened his arms in greeting. "Thank you all for coming. We are here today to say farewell to one of our best friends and to a true humanitarian."

Several people in the audience nodded and there were a few "Amens" said aloud. The Reverend looked distinguished, Sandi thought, and a bit like the television minister Robert Schuller. Rev. Savelle had the finely-combed gray hair, glistening under the lights of the church, and a deep voice that boomed confidence yet at the same time reassurance to the crowd. "In Shakespeare's play, Julius Caesar, Anthony says he comes to bury Caesar, not to praise him, then proceeds to praise him. We come today to remember and not just praise our late friend Dr. Wes. For all his achievements, Dr. Wes remained a humble man. He would not like a litany of his accomplishments during the eulogy, and besides, when he was making his will, he specifically asked me to keep the ceremony short so that there would not be time to list all he has done for the human race." Sandi smiled. A few laughs came from others in the congregation. That did, indeed, sound like her father.

"Dr. Wes was blessed with a can-do personality and a high intelligence. He used those gifts to bless humanity. He helped countless patients during his time as a doctor and, with his oil ventures, he has set this nation on a path to energy independence. The practice of 'fracking', which Dr. Wes championed, has opened up vast oil fields for this nation. In a short time, we will no longer be dependent on nations who subsidize terrorists for our oil. This will be a tremendous benefit to the United States." Again, there were nods of agreement.

"Many people, and perhaps some in foreign countries, do not like fracking. Dr. Wes and his associates were known to even receive death threats from time to time. Wesley mentioned to me once that he never took such threats seriously unless they were in good English and contained good spelling. "You'd be amazed," he said, "at how many would-be, amateur killers are atrocious spellers. However, when the company gets a threat that is in good English and has every word spelled correctly, we do notify the authorities.""

In spite of herself, Sandi laughed again. That was a running joke with her father. He was often amused at how incoherent some of his hate mail was.

"But that shows a trait of Dr. Wes. Once he believed a project or an idea had merit and was the right thing to do, there was no stopping him. He was like a hound on the trail of a fox, ready to overcome any obstacle and solve any problem to achieve his goal. He once said to me, "There are no problems; simply solutions we haven't found yet." Dr.

Wes certainly found plenty of solutions and then went on to his next goal."

Sandi noticed her stepmother, Maggie, whispering sweetly to Dr. Matt. He smiled. The sight of it repelled her. Sandi glared at the two until Maggie had finished and turned her face toward Rev. Savelle again.

"Dr. Wes achieved something that was exceedingly rare. He was extraordinary successful in two vastly different fields – medicine and the oil business. He was not only a skilled, caring physician, but also an astute, ethical businessman. In both fields, he made innovations and was creative. Any businessman, at times, needs to be tough and decisive, which he was, but he was also gentle and caring with his patients. Even though he may have had a hundred things on his plate and fifty things to make decisions about, no doctor had a better bedside manner than Dr. Wes Hunter. When he spoke to you, it seemed that he had nowhere to go and could spend all the time in the world with you.

But the two prizes of his life, what he was most proud of, were not his achievements in medicine or in the energy field, but his children, Sandi and Bill. Together with his grandchildren, they were the apples of his eye, vastly more important to him than either medicine or oil.

Rev. Savelle opened his arms again, as if he was about to give the benediction. "We all have wonderful stories about Dr. Wes and I could spend the entire afternoon telling some of them. But Dr. Wes told me bluntly that he did not want a long service. He thought that Stewart and Eldon would want to get back on the golf course!"

Steward, Eldon, Sandi and a few others gave a brusque laugh at the statement.

"So we are going to let you get to the golf course. I thank you all for coming and for being here today as we say our final farewell to our dear friend, Dr. Wes. He left the world a better place. Let us hope we can all say that when our journeys are over."

There was a brief reception after the eulogy in the church's hallway. The short, ruddy man from Hunter Oil walked up to Sandy and offered his condolences. "Kurt Reynolds," he said. "I was one of your father's vice-presidents."

"Of course, Mr. Reynolds," Sandi said. "I should have remembered your name."

"No reason to, ma'am. We only met once but I did want to tell you how sorry I am at your father's passing. He was a wonderful man."

"Yes, he was."

She turned and looked toward the other oil associates of her father. "Mr. Reynolds, could you tell me the names of the others? I'd like to send them a personal thank you card."

"Certainly."

"The woman. I don't believe I know her."

"Jane Dawson. She handles communications and public relations for the company. We are very fortunate to have her. She is an immensely likeable woman and is at home during television interviews or on talk shows speaking about the business."

"And the tall man beside her?"

"Vince Attaway. Been with the company for about fifteen years and was very helpful to your father."

"Yes, I recall the name. I think I've met him too, but with all that's been going on, I didn't remember him at first."

"We all had great respect for your father and for the entire Hunter family."

"Thank you."

When Reynolds moved away, Sandi again focused on Dr. Ross and her stepmother. They were deep in conversation. A conversation that, to her, indicated they were more than friends. She bristled with indignation. Her father was an adult, so she'd never told him of her reservations about his second marriage. For a hard-driving businessman, sometimes Dr. Wes could be too trusting. Sandi moved over to her brother and tapped him on the shoulder. "Bill, where's Dr. Knowland? He's not here."

Her brother had a glass of water in his hand. He sipped it before answering. "You haven't heard the latest?" he whispered.

"No. I guess not."

"There has been something of a falling-out between Brian and Dad. And something of a mini-scandal. Hospital is trying to keep it quiet, of course."

Sandi blinked and gasped. This was news to her. "A minor disagreement or something more serious?" she asked.

Her brother frowned. "More serious. The Ethics Review Board may be convened over some allegations about Brian. He denies all charges. He wanted Dad to use his influence to quash the matter, but Dad refused. He said things needed to be aired, but said the Ethics Board would of course give Brian a chance to defend himself."

"That does sound serious." Sandi turned her head as another mourner came by to shake hands with her and her brother and offer condolences.

She gave Bill a hasty smile. "Obviously this isn't the time, but I want to hear more about this when we can talk privately."

Dr. Bill nodded.

Marian Hinkley came over and offered her condolences again. She must have been a beautiful woman once, Sandi thought. But now the eyes looked sad and lines criss-crossed her face. Sandi wondered if she'd had a hard life.

* * *

Outside the church building, two federal agents watched silently from their car. Donald Everett, tall, slender man with an aquiline nose and narrow chin, smashed a cigarette in a cup holder he used as an ashtray. "I need to give up smoking, but it's difficult on jobs like this." He paused, waiting for his partner to reply. Without a word, Art Steely stared at him. For a moment, Everett looked toward the building "This is a waste of time, but it's not like we had anything else to do."

"You keep smoking and we'll be watching your funeral soon," Steely added. He was almost a health nut. He exercised regularly and watched his diet. It was irony that he was paired with Donald Everett, who was a chain smoker.

"Why do you think we're doing this?" Everett asked.

"I'm assuming someone in our higher echelons has a suspicion the good doctor did not die of natural causes, nor from a fall."

"That's what I was thinking. The guy was rich, and rich people have enemies. A lot of friends too, of course, but definitely a few enemies." Everett paused then turned to look at his partner. "Think the Badger had anything to do with this?"

"Possibly. The evidence we've seen is sketchy but odd enough to prompt a few inquiries. We've seen a few terrorist attacks in the nation but, if our suspicions bear out, it'd be the first time any terrorist group have targeted an individual."

"Yes, but there's always a first time," Everett said. "Maybe a new era has opened in our war on terrorism. If the reports about the Badger are true—"

"That's a big IF."

"There've been rumors and a reported sighting," said Everett, lighting another cigarette and keeping his gaze on the church.

"We get rumors and reported sightings all the time," Steely commented. "Ninety-five percent of them are pure fiction."

Everett blew out some smoke and give Art a somewhat wry smile. "But there's always that other five percent."

"But most murders, if this was a murder, are more… personal. Chances are it was a business rival, or an old girlfriend. You can never discount an old girlfriend," Steely added.

"You are cynical, Art. Very cynical."

"As are you, Donald," Steely replied.

"Yes, well I've been married three times." He showed a weary smile. "Of course, I can't blame all the problems on my ex-wives. I've come to the decision that I am simply not good husband material. My wives have also come to that conclusion. Besides, sometimes cynicism helps in our profession. We are not exactly tracking the best in mankind, now are we?"

Steely pointed towards the church. "Those we track down aren't generally the best, but Dr. Hunter might have been. Ever seen his resume? The man was incredibly impressive. How many people have had such successful careers in two different professions? The man was a genius."

"Yes, but even geniuses have skeletons in his closet. Most people do."

"Well, he didn't have three wives. Only two."

Everett laughed. "That's true. Sometimes, though, it's not advisable to be so effective in your work. You can attract the attention of very nasty people. Although I don't think the Badger objected to Dr. Hunter's medical career. It was the oil business that got his attention. If, in fact, the Badger is around. I'm still betting that if it was murder, then it was done for personal, rather than political reasons."

Steely shook his head. "Darn strange world. It's more acceptable if cases are cut-and-dried. The killer is an ex-lover, a current wife, a disgruntled greedy relative. Those are the easy ones. Nowadays you have to check out every rumor in the wind, and there are rumors galore."

They straightened as men and women filed out of the church. A few last words were said, then the individuals walked to their cars. "Looks like it's over. No surprises. Not that we really expected any," Everett murmured. "Another dead end."

Chapter 3

Los Angeles, California

Four Weeks Later

Modern technology and the 21st century had damaged the honorable if at one time dusty profession of private investigator, Sandi Burnside thought. She had been a double major in college, with the second being in criminal justice. She had upset any number of professors by her enjoyment of old mysteries, especially those of Raymond Chandler and his private detective Philip Marlowe. While Chandler had received some critical recognition by a few academics, Sandi's professors were not among his fans. But she still pictured a private detective's office as being essentially seedy, with dust on both the desk and on the files, and cigarette smoke rising languidly toward the ceiling. She could still picture Humphrey Bogart playing Spade in the old movies, a cigarette butt between his fingers. Bogart's gravel-like voice was perfect for Marlowe. And while Bogart looked clean, his office hadn't seen a vacuum cleaner for decades.

Located on the third floor of a business high-rise in northern Los Angeles, the office of Sandi's ex-husband,

Harry Burnside, looked nothing like those pictured in books. He still lived in LA, although Sandi had moved to Elm Grove. The complex's cleaning staff came in three times a week to dust and scrub and wash and do anything else needed to keep it spotless. Bogart's office did not, of course, have computers but her husband had two monitors on his desk. Harry had no cigarette between his fingers although he did enjoy a bourbon at the end of the day.

Looking neither seedy nor disheveled, Harry Burnside wore a clean, blue business suit with a blue tie. He was a slender man with a pale face and a gray mustache that Sandi thought — even if they were divorced — made him look distinguished. Gray was invading his black hair too. But the one good thing about her ex-husband — well, perhaps there was more than one good thing, she reflected — was that he didn't have any pretentions. He didn't color his hair, but took pride in the gray, and although he wasn't a particularly religious man, he often quoted the line from Proverbs, that gray hair is a crown of splendor attained by a life of righteousness. He was also exceptional in his job and that was what she needed. That was another good point about Harry, Sandi thought. She opened the door to his office and smiled.

"Hello, Harry."

He stood up and walked toward her. He kissed her cheek and they hugged briefly. "Come in. Please have a seat." She eased into a comfortable office chair which, with its green cushions, looked more like a recliner. "I think my clients should be comfortable," Burnside said, when he noted her reaction. "Sometimes they're talking about difficult subjects so I want them to relax."

It would take more than a chair to relax her, Sandi thought. In her mid-forties, she had retained her striking beauty. At five-seven, she hadn't gained a pound in twenty years. The blonde hair, cut short, shone, as did the remarkably blue eyes, which were alive with intelligence. Raised with money, she didn't have to cultivate charm or manners. They seemed to come naturally to her. Both she and Harry took great pride in their two college-aged children. Mark, a senior, had declared an interest in sciences and planned to go into research. Catherine, their daughter, would enter medical school within the year, following in her grandfather's footsteps.

Nodding, Sandi waited until Harry was seated then said, "I'm concerned about the circumstances surrounding Dad's death and I would like for you to help me with the investigation."

"I guessed that was the reason for the visit?" Harry asked.

"Yes…Yes. Most definitely."

Burnside raised his eyebrows. "Sandi, the authorities would leave no stone unturned. To us, he was family, but to the world he was Dr. Wesley Charles Hunter, prominent surgeon, CEO of the Elm Grove Medical Center and also noted businessman. I'm sure the authorities checked everything. As I understand it, there was nothing to indicate foul play."

She shook her head. "I don't care, Harry. I can't believe Dad fell down the stairs. You knew him. He was larger than life. A man like that doesn't die by tripping and hitting his head."

"Accidents happen, Sandi."

"Not to Dr. Wes. Not to my father. I know he was sixty-five and people do slow down when they age, but not him. He was still running full-steam."

"And he might have been running full-steam when he tripped and fell. The fact that he was Dr. Wesley Hunter doesn't exclude him from the routine calamities of life. You hear about that case six months ago? The rich Oregon timber-man? What was he worth? Six hundred million? Wheeler-dealer. Investor. And most of his investments paid off. So he gets out of his large bathtub one night, slips on the floor. The toilet lid is up and he slams his head on the porcelain bowl. He's killed instantly. Not the best way to die perhaps, but slips are a part of life."

"I'm still not satisfied. Harry, I don't have any hard evidence but something about Dad's death just smells bad. I'd like to hire you to take a second look at it. Go over the police evidence, the records, everything and see if you spot anything amiss."

Burnside put his elbows on his desk and leaned forward. "Sandi, I have no objections to taking your money. You're rich and you can afford it. And you're still the mother of my children, he wanted to add. But I've got to be honest with you and say I think you're on a wild goose chase. I don't think the police would have overlooked anything, especially not when the deceased is as prominent as your father was. I know something about the police up in Elm Grove. Some are friends of mine and they do good work."

"I know about your law enforcement contacts and I'm counting on that." She edged forward and drum the table with her fingers. "I don't think they put enough credence in

34

the death threats Dad had received. He had any number of people angry enough to kill."

In addition to his medical practice, Dr. Wes had inherited a small, but still impressive, oil company which had been established by his father. But he was also among the first to recognize the importance of fracking," and he heavily invested in the new technology. The North Dakota boom due to fracking was partly fueled by companies Wes Hunter had a controlling interest in. Radical ecologists had picketed his speeches on several occasions and he had often debated with environmentalists who claimed that fracking was a danger to both nature and to individuals. But Hunter, with his scientific background, easily bested his opponents.

"Sandi, please believe me when I say I do not dismiss such threats. Anyone who gets an email that says the sender is going to kill him should immediately go to the police. But it's also true that almost anyone in public life nowadays gets such threats. This isn't new. When Jerry Falwell formed the Moral Majority thirty or forty years ago, he got up to 200 death threats a month. Thankfully, no one ever attempted to carry them out. The authorities looked at those threats and concluded that there was no real substance to them. Threats only."

"I'm not so sure. The radical environmentalists now are akin to the violent protestors of the sixties. And they bombed anyone they disliked. They were self-righteous and didn't mind killing anyone who disagreed with them," Sandi said.

"Your politics are showing, honey."

"Perhaps, but what I said was true. We do have radical environmental groups in this part of the country and they've carried out violent acts too. Those tree-huggers are not only nuts, they are murderous nuts."

"Two or three are. Maybe more," Burnside said. "But the Earth Liberation Front has been the group responsible for most of those crimes and they've stayed away from the fracking battles. They're more concerned with trees and forests, at least for now. I know policemen and FBI people, now retired, who were serving in the sixties and seventies. Some of those street protest radicals were dangerous. They were pathological in their hatred of the nation and of anyone they disliked. Policemen of that day have a lot of stories that were never covered in the national press. I don't discount your concerns, Sandi. But there's no evidence linking any of these people to the death of your father."

"They hated his politics."

"And they love the politics of your stepmother."

"Please don't mention her. She's a money-hungry shark and a snotty little poseur. Wish Dad had never married her. You know—" Sandi was tempted to let Harry know how she felt about her stepmother. Instead, she sighed deeply and let the matter drop.

"She was in France," Burnside said quickly, "Which is a pretty good alibi. She had to fly home when informed of your dad's death. Although I suppose she could have hired someone." Burnside stared at his former wife.

For a moment she stared back, then threw up her arms, as if in surrender. "Okay, Maggie probably didn't kill Dad. Despite the fact that I don't like the woman and thought Dad made a terrible choice for his second wife, I have to admit I don't think she's a murderer. " She was silent for a moment, then added, "But I could be wrong."

The detective had to chuckle. "As I understand it, your dad's estate was hammered out in detail by his meticulous attorneys. The bulk of the estate goes to you and your brother and while Margaret gets a hefty settlement, she's not that much better off with your father dead than alive. She had access to more of his fortune when he was alive."

Sandi frowned. "Yes, I think that's true. Still, she was not, as she sometimes claims, a child of a wealthy, established family from back east. Her family was upper middle class but didn't have the pedigree she sometimes pretends."

"I don't have that problem. My old man was a drunk and I always told everyone he was a drunk. The only good thing about him is he wasn't a mean drunk. In fact, he became rather mellow when he was downing all the beers. That was the second good point. At least his alcoholism didn't cost too much.

He always liked the cheap stuff." He shook his head. "But mom still loved him and missed him for a long time after he passed on." He leaned back in his chair. "Sandi, does your brother agree with you about this endeavor?"

She nodded. "He does, although he's not as passionate about it as I am. I think he believes Dad's death was accidental but he doesn't mind having a detective take a second look at all the evidence, just to make sure."

"I will do that for you but I can't promise any startling revelations."

"But you do have contacts in both state and federal law enforcement agencies," Sandi said. "That might help. Is it true the FBI had a man looking over this case?"

Harry nodded. "Due to his petroleum businesses and his medical expertise, your father had international contacts. He had several Chinese physicians tour his facility last year and he attended oil conferences that had representatives from dozens of countries on four continents. The FBI was curious but found nothing to contradict the official report."

"But I still think falling down the stairs is just a little too pat. Besides, it's a bit strange that Marian didn't see or hear anything, don't you think?"

Harry gave her a blank stare. "Marian?"

"Marian Hinkley. The housekeeper."

"Oh, for a moment I forgot her name. No, I don't think it was strange. Your father had a huge house. The estimated time of death was between eleven-thirty and one in the morning. Marian was on the other side of the house, asleep. She wouldn't have heard anything."

"I still wonder about her story, though."

"Sandi, she checked on your father at about ten-thirty. He didn't want anything, so she went to bed. Because she was in the house, she has to be a suspect, but I see no motive for her to kill your father. She received a modest sum in his will, but nothing worth murdering for."

Sandi frowned. "It's doubtful, yes. But I've moved back into the house after Dad's death, and Marian seems…just a bit odd in her behavior. Edgy. Nervous."

"Sandi, her previous employer died on her and she discovered the body. That might keep one uneasy for a couple of weeks. Especially when there's been a police investigation during most of that time."

Sandi was silent for a moment. "Maybe. But there's something else. I know something that is not in the official reports."

"Know what?" Harry asked, although something in Sandi's tone suggested that whatever it was, Harry might not want to know about it.

"Dad had several email accounts. One for his medical practice, one for his business and one as his personal account. He also had a fourth account, which he used for very private, very confidential matters, both business and personal. Only a few people allegedly knew that private email address."

"Yes, but privacy nowadays is almost non-existent."

"Very true. A few days before Dad's death, someone hacked into the account."

"That happens."

"And someone sent him a warning," Sandi said.

"A death threat?"

Sandi shook her head. "No, not a threat. A warning. It told him to be very careful and that he should hire a bodyguard. And the message finished with the sentence, "Someone wants you dead"."

Burnside's untidy appearance indicated a lack in his habitual neatness. He wasn't usually a sloppy dresser, but today he was wearing a pastel shirt with a dark blue tie. Slowly, Sandi realized her ex-husband had snapped to attention, although he was still sitting down. "Did you tell the police this?" he asked.

"I didn't know about it until two days ago when I was going over some of Dad's old files. But the police already knew about the death threats. I figured they wouldn't put any more credence in this email than they had in the others. But this one wasn't from someone who threatened to kill dad. If was from someone telling him to be careful."

Burnside brought his hand up and wrapped it around his chin. "That is curious. Were you able trace the email?"

"No. Obviously on our business side we have export techies but the email led to a dead end."

"And that was the entire message? The mailer didn't say why your father should be careful or who wanted him dead?"

"No," Sandi said.

"So it could have been another crank?"

"Could have. But it appeared two days before dad died."

Harry shook his head. "But there's still no motive to kill your father, not one I can see. Things were going well at the medical center, weren't they? No serious knock-down arguments between your father and Dr. Ross?"

Dr. Matthew Ross was the director of the neurosurgery department at the Elm Grove Medical Center and the family's private physician.

"As far as I knew, they were getting along fine," Sandi said quietly.

Harry opened his hands, palms up, as if in resignation. "Well there you have it. No real motive. No evidence of foul play. But I will nose around and ask a couple of questions if you like. Things have been a bit slow lately and I could use a job."

40

Sandi reached into her purse and brought out a checkbook. A pen was in her left hand. "You take checks, don't you?"

"I am incredibly old-fashioned when it comes to money. Cash, debit cards or electronic transfers are welcome. I even accept cash. I'm not picky."

She handed him the check. "That should pay for about two weeks of work."

When he saw the numbers, his eyebrows shifted up. "That will pay for travel and the rented apartment when I come to Elm Grove."

"The children will be happy to see you again on their winter break."

"It will be good to see them too." He waved the check in the air again. "This will definitely pay for two weeks and more. But I might hit a dead end in three days."

"Then keep the money anyway. I just want to know I did everything possible to allay my suspicions about Dad's death."

"As you noted, I do have contacts in law enforcement – a lot of contacts. I'll start making calls and pulling in some favors."

"I appreciate it, Harry."

"If anything significant pops up, I'll let you know."

"I can email and scan you a lot of background on Dad. It may help the investigation."

When Sandi left, Harry looked at the check for a few moments. He had been married to a very wealthy woman but, when the divorce came, he hadn't taken any of her money. He hadn't felt right doing so. A little old-fashioned chivalry, perhaps. Probably out of date in this age. He frowned. Maybe both of them would think differently about the divorce now; neither had found anybody else. He also wondered if the real reason he'd taken the case was to obtain a legitimate reason to meet and talk to Sandi again. Dr. Wes was a high-profile entrepreneur, but Harry failed to see why anyone would want to kill him. He doubted he'd find anything to contradict the police report but he would give the case his best. He owned that to Sandi. He owed it to any client.

After lunch, he received an email from Sandi. Although he knew a great deal about her father, he decided he should carefully read the bio and the backup information – after all, Dr. Wes might have become involved in many projects since he had stopped being the man's son-in-law. Harry needed enough pieces of the puzzle in place to convince Sandi that it wasn't murder. Probable cause took work, sometimes a whole lot of work.

Chapter 4

Los Angeles, California

It was very late in the evening, and Harry was still scrutinizing the emails and scanned reports that Sandi had sent him on Dr. Wesley Hunter. Dr. Wes had been born with an almost-silver spoon in his mouth, but his innate talent and abilities had allowed him to create a silver dinnerware set. His parents, Patrick and Olivia Hunter, had emigrated to the USA and settled in Boston when Wes was only five years old. Patrick came from a long line of Irish and Italian descendants. He never remembered which side was which. Patrick had worked initially as a laborer and vowed someday that they would buy some land and settle down, which they finally did, in South Dakota where land was very cheap. Within five years of saving his money, he was able to purchase one thousand acres in the north-western part of the state to start a cattle farm. Two years later, he'd found oil on his land and had invested wisely in petroleum. This gave the Hunters a hefty income that paid for Wes's schooling and a lifestyle they'd never thought possible.

Blessed with a high IQ and an affable personality, Wes kept his hand in oil dealings while finishing medical school. Irritated by the number of bureaucratic rules he had to deal with in medical centers, he created his own – the humbly-named Elm Grove Medical Facility, which had become regionally, if not nationally known. A little-known facet of the center was its genetic research facility, which made a few people, both on the secular left and the religious right, nervous. In his investigation, Burnside mentally noted that there had been some threats sent to the genetic facility and a few to Dr. Wes himself.

Harry supposed that the prospect of tinkering with man's DNA just scared some people; they wanted it ruled out of bounds. There was a small office of AGEN (Anti-Genetic Engineering Network) in Elm Grove, set up there because of the genetic facility at the Elm Grove Medical Center. There had been a few small protests and a blog established a blog in which opponents criticized the center and Dr. Wes. But none of the members had ever participated in a violent protest. They had links to Greenpeace and other organizations that shared their views, but members had not been threatening in any manner.

Harry did not want to believe that there was so much information on his father-in-law. Still, one might ask them a few questions. Some information he knew already, so he just skipped most of the detail. There was no doubt the good doctor was a humanitarian. He had subsidized medical facilities for the poor and sick and contributed annual hefty sums to religious organizations helping the needy. A first marriage had produced two children, Sandi and William. Sandi had veered away from both the medical field and entrepreneurship, preferring instead to marry, move to Los Angeles and begin a successful career as a criminal attorney

Harry read about Bill's medical career and his resentment to Sandi being the favored sibling. Burnside had seen this resentment played out several times while still married to Sandi, but it had never, as it easily could have, devolved into malice and hatred.

William loved his sister but still carried that resentment from his childhood – towards his father too, to a degree. Perhaps because he'd known that he couldn't achieve more than his father in medicine or business, the resentment had often come out on the golf course. Every time when teeing off, William had been a passionate competitor, always trying to beat his father on the links. Burnside, when he was still in the family, had played numerous rounds with both father and son. He recognized the fierce dedication to winning that William had. Dr. Wes had never seemed to notice, or perhaps just pretended not to. As luck or fate would have it, Dr. Wes was a good golfer too and William lost as many games as he won.

My father-in-law was a genius, Harry thought, scanning the email. He'd recognize the immense importance of fracking. Harry had seen that Wes might not only revolutionize the petroleum industry but the entire world, and it seemed he was being proved right. With the success of the fracking industry in North Dakota, Saudi Arabia was sweating bullets. So were a few other Arab nations. While their fiscal empire did not entirely depend on America, the United States was always a ready buyer of oil. And because their oil supplies were thought to be unlimited, the Arab nations continually pumped black gold and stuffed the revenues into their bank accounts. Even though they were rich, many spent so much that their nations were in debt or at least teetering on a fiscal razor's edge. A sudden loss of oil revenues might cause serious economic and social problems for them.

This is interesting. My children have a grandfather I wish I had. I don't blame Sandi for not being able to rest until she knows the truth. Harry stood up and stretched. It was getting late. He looked out of the window – no answers there. He was glad to be leaving LA, at least for a while. The daily traffic wore him down. Besides, the city had begun to run down. At one time the streets were clean and smooth. Wear and tear and more than a few rough spots now crowded the streets. It would be nice to get back to a small – or at least smaller – city again.

He returned to his desk and studied the anonymous email threats made by American anti-fracking protestors. Their environmental allegations against the policy were without merit and scientifically invalid. Fracking, when properly employed, was a safe method of extracting shale oil from the ground. It promised an economic boom for the nation and high-paying jobs for hundreds of thousands of workers. The anti-fracking fanatics, though, had a hatred for gas and oil, believing the products polluted the environment. They preferred solar and wind power but, as yet, those energy sources were not financially viable and perhaps they never would be.

In the vitriolic emails, Dr. Wes was accused of killing the environment and killing the Earth, thus causing hundreds of thousands of human deaths. Fanatics can get shrill, Harry noted. He thought of the European professor who, a few

46

months before, had called for the execution of scientists who were climate change skeptics. Could some random wacko in this region feel the same way as the European professor and decide to carry out the executions starting with Dr. Wes, who had expressed some caution with the climate change theories? Possibly. Every movement has its extremist and fanatics. But if so, he was a careful assassin. Political fanatics like to bomb people or shoot them. Burnside was a history buff and, off the top of his head, could think of no political assassin who broke necks. So perhaps the killer – if there was a killer – was closer to home. Yet he wasn't aware of any personal hatred toward Dr. Wes.

In Harry's experience, on the death of a rich man, the wife is usually a 'person of interest'. But the second wife of Dr. Wes, Margaret Emily Boston, was in France when he died. He remembered Sandi giving him this information earlier There was no friction that he knew of between the doctor and his wife, who seemed to love him very much. Maggie was a prominent supporter of liberal causes, so there was some tension between her and the much more conservative Sandi, but none between her and her husband. Besides, most of Wes's estate had been left to his children and grandchildren; Maggie received a very generous settlement, but the control of Dr. Wes's many enterprises passed to his children, not to his second wife.

Dead end, Harry thought. Dead end and he was only an hour or so into two weeks worth of work. He suppressed the thought that Sandi had overpaid him. Tremendously overpaid him. But since she was there, he would leave immediately for Elm Grove. What am I waiting for? No reason to waste time.

Chapter 5

Elm Grove, Nevada

Six Weeks Later

"Yes, I agreed with Sandi to go along with this but at the same time I have no real enthusiasm for independent detective work. I have no reason to doubt the official police report," Dr. William Hunter said emphatically. He spoke quickly, as if needing to get the words out of his mouth. He had a slight resemblance to his father. His nose, chin and elongated face were all shared by both father and son. But whereas his father also had a friendly and sunny charisma, Dr. Bill was more aloof and had a cool exterior.

"But you didn't object when Sandi wanted to hire me?" Harry asked.

"No, but there was no reason to. You are my brother-in-law – or at least you were. Sandi would have hired you even if I did object. I saw no reason to start a quarrel. The relations between my sister and I have been strained, as I'm sure you know. I'm trying to repair them, so agreeing with her seemed the proper thing to do. I'm sure she was more distraught about Dad's death than I was. She was always the favored sibling. And she is female. She's never had to walk in Dad's shadow of Dr. Wes all these years."

"You've done all right and established your own life and your own reputation," Harry said.

Dr. Bill sighed. "No one, at least in this area of the country, can compete with Dr. Wesley Hunter. He is – or rather was – an idol." He shrugged. "But that's neither here nor there. On the matter at hand, I can give you no information I didn't tell to the police. Dad's death looks to be a tragic accident. Nothing more."

Harry shifted in his seat. He had talked often with Bill The man was blessed with a razor-shape mind, was near didactic and possessed an irony that often gave way to a remarkable sense of humor. He also cared deeply about his little charges. He had garnered more respect from doctors and nurses than even his father did. What he hated most in life was giving the parents of his patients bad news. At those distressing times, he could turn angry and become 'Dr. Hyde' to others. But he knew his own character and generally, when he was in a Dr. Hyde mood, stayed away from people.

When Harry was a member of the family, he had never been able to like Sandi's brother. Although he was undoubtedly a skilled pediatric surgeon, there was a coldness in the man's personality. Harry remembered some of the golf matches between father and son and their often tense relationship with each other. His thoughts shifted. No, it was unlikely that tangled family relationships had anything to do with Dr. Wes's death. At times, Bill disdained the human race. I wonder if the doctor had any close friends or colleagues. Why did Bill choose to work with children?

"If it wasn't an accident, would you have any suspects in mind?" The doctor smirked and gave a harsh laugh.

"Is that funny to you?" Harry asked. Hunter picked up a pen and twirled it in his fingers, like a gambler rolling cards.

"As a matter of fact, yes." Bill chuckled. "The obvious suspect would be my father's doctor, Dr. Matthew Ross, noted neurosurgeon and my father's personal physician." The comment shocked Harry. He did not particularly like William Hunter but he respected him as a doctor and he had never known the doctor, whatever his other faults, to be malicious or, for that matter, to be less than truthful.

"Why do you say that?"

Bill tapped the pen on the table. "Oh, yes. Dad married Maggie after you'd left the family. It's not generally known around the medical center but Dr. Ross was – and perhaps still is – in love with Maggie. It crushed him when she married Dad. I'm sure if Maggie had agreed, he would have run away with her, far away from Elm Grove and the Hunter name. That's one reason why he never remarried after his divorce. He's still pining for Maggie."

"I gather Maggie didn't feel the same way about him."

"I wouldn't jump to that conclusion. But I don't converse with my stepmother much, and certainly not about romantic matters. To answer your next question, Matthew has become a friend of mine and we often play golf together. He's a very good player and we've got to talking about a lot of things. I've known he's loved Maggie since before the marriage. To be honest, I was hoping she felt the same way

51

about him. But perhaps she was enthralled by Dad's money and fame. Of course that's what Sandi thinks. She believes Maggie married for money, not love."

"But you don't think Dr. Ross would be a suspect, do you?"

Hunter shrugged again. "Who knows what jealousy might drive a man to? Dad had it easy for most of his life. Yes, he worked hard and he possessed considerable business and medical talents. He did a lot of good works in his life. But life came easy for him. Maggie was easy for him. He's never nourished resentments because he had nothing to resent. For a man, such as Dr. Ross, who had to struggle all his life and then has to see the woman he loves marry a man who has breezed through life like a sail boat with a gentle wind behind it…well, it might gall you." Are you that good a friend of Dr. Ross? Burnside thought. So good a friend you figure him as a possible murderer?

"I will tell you something, Harry, and I assume you'll keep it confidential. Dad wasn't a man to talk about his private life but recently he let something slip. Perhaps he was thinking out loud but I just happened to be in the room."

"And? Is it something worth repeating?"

"Yes and no. I'm not sure. But Maggie takes several trips to France every year, and my father knew that they were times when Dr. Ross was out of the country too. He also visited other parts of Europe."

"A long way for a rendezvous. A mere coincidence, perhaps?"

"Perhaps, but I don't think so. They have the money for it."

Dr. Ross shifted in his chair. "Of course I'm not saying Matt killed Dad, or even thought about it. I'm just saying you never know what jealousy and resentment can breed."

"True enough," Harry said.

"However, it's also true that he doesn't have an alibi."

"How do you know that?"

"The night before Dad died, we were at a social event. Mr. and Mrs. Walter Alisester hosted a little party just for the fun of it. Dad never liked social gatherings. He was too busy with other things so, as usual, he sent his best but declined to actually show up himself. I was there and so was Matt. But I noticed that Matt left at about nine. Since he lives alone I assume he doesn't have an alibi for that evening. I stayed until about eleven, and then left. So Matt had both motive and opportunity. But I still don't see him as homicidal."

Burnside shook his head. He wondered again what type of friend William Hunter was. Not the kind I would want, he thought. Hunter twirled the pen around again in his fingers. "But when you talk to Matt, you can ask him about Dad's headaches – he's had them off and on for some time now. That's another reason I doubt anyone killed him. He'd been having severe headaches for about three weeks, but he just shrugged them off. Sometimes doctors ignore their own advice and they make the worst patients. But I have no idea whether the headaches were migraines or something worse.

Many people have migraines when they're younger but tend to lessen or even disappear with age. Only a few individuals get migraines as they get older but it's possible. Or it could have been a symptom of something much more serious. Say an aneurysm. I think that Matt urged Dad to have some tests done but he keep saying that he was too busy or some such excuse. When I first heard that Dad had died, I immediately thought it was from an aneurysm."

Harry nodded. "Besides Matt, any other enemies? Or friends with resentments?"

"Nope, can't think of anyone. Of course, once in a while those Greenpeace freaks send a nasty email. I've even been confronted myself once or twice by a wide-eyed protestor claiming I'm destroying the Earth. But my stock in the oil company is very low. If I'm destroying the Earth, I'm only destroying a very small piece of it."

Harry thanked him and stood up. Dr. Wes could light up a room when he walked into it, and make everyone feel important. An aura of friendliness had surrounded him like a cloud. But perhaps such charm, like schizophrenia, skips a generation. Maybe it was silly or maybe he was getting paranoid or maybe he was letting not his dislike of Dr. Bill, but questions about him become more worrisome than they should. But he thought he might check with the hosts of the party and see if William Hunter had indeed waited until eleven before leaving the party that evening.

Even if he had, of course, that wasn't a perfect alibi. Dr. Wes had been killed between three and six o'clock in the morning. That would have given a resentful son time enough to drive over to his father's house and...

But you have no evidence, Harry thought. Just a bad feeling.

Chapter 6

Summerlin, Nevada

Seven Weeks Later

Matthew Ross had Wednesday afternoon off, so he was on the Pine Ridge Country Club driving range working on his slice. After the recent storm, a warm weather front had moved in. He wore a bright yellow shirt with a blue sweater. Harry heard a smack as the red three-wood knocked the golf ball. The ball zoomed into the air but swerved left. "Darn. Thought I'd corrected my swing but my slice is back. It practically puts me in the rough off every tee," he said, looking at Burnside. "In a couple of years, maybe next year, I'll retire and work on my golf game all day long."

He teed up another ball, sighed and looked down the range. The two-hundred yard marker was a square green sign with white numbers on it. Ross swung again but this time kept his elbow in and his head down. A solid whack sounded when the club hit the ball, knocking the tee out of the ground. It flipped over several times then landed softly on the mat. The ball soared straight. Instead of slicing, it drew right slightly as it sailed past the green, fading to the left. "Yes, if I can hit two-ten, two-fifteen with a three-wood, it's a great drive for me." He reached down to put another ball on the tee. "So what can I do for you, Harry?"

"I'm investigating Dr. Wes's death."

Dr. Matt jerked to attention. "Really? But the police had officially declared that an accident."

"Sandi wants a second opinion."

Ross frowned. "She would – she was always a daddy's girl. Her old man could do no wrong in her eyes. She probably thought he would live forever, which no man does. Probably thought he was perfect too. Which no man is either."

Harry noticed the bitterness in Ross's voice. "A lot of people say Dr. Wes came close."

"Yeah, right," Ross replied. His next drive veered sharply to the left again, dropping to the ground well short of the 200-yard marker.

"Didn't mean to hurt your game, Matt," Harry said.

Dr. Matt frowned, dropped the three-wood to the ground and rested his hands on the shaft. "Like all Type-A people, my colleague could be exasperating at times. But through the decades he was a good friend. You know we went to medical school together?"

Harry listened attentively, and when Matt asked the question, he shook his head and said, "It means you're about the same age."

Matt threw his head back and chuckled loudly. "I'm a year younger. But Wes was brilliant back then, really stood out in the class. There was no question that he'd have a distinguished career. Few of us knew about the oil interests back then. But he was as good in business as he was in medicine."

"Any enemies?"

Dr. Matt snickered and made a practice swing. The club swooshed through the air. "Wes was the salt of the earth. How can you imagine he had any enemies?"

"I noticed the sarcasm in your voice, Matt. Perhaps this is the time I should ask you a question. I'll be blunt. Are you in love with Maggie?"

The club slipped out of his grip. It landed on the ground and bounced once. At first the doctor looked defiant and angry. Then his countenance changed and became stoic. He walked five steps and picked up the club. Pacing back, he slipped it into his golf bag, and then turned to face Burnside. His tone was soft but strong. "Yes, I've been in love with Maggie for years. I was in love with her before she married Wes. I hoped she would marry me instead."

"Maybe she will now."

He shook his head. "We haven't discussed it. Too soon after the funeral. Might look a bit strange, getting married to Wes's widow such a short time after the funeral." He twisted the corner of mouth.

"I guess that might make me a suspect. So do you think I killed Wes to marry Maggie?"

"Just asking the questions I need to ask, Matt."

"Let's go in and get a drink, Harry." The two sat at a small round table in the lounge. A glass of beer sat in front of Burnside. Ross had his fingers around a bourbon on the rocks. He sipped it. "To be honest, there were times when I wanted to kill Wes. He could be arrogant, you know?

Don't get me wrong – he had huge humanitarian instincts and acted on many of them. He did a lot of good in the world. But every man has flaws and he could certainly be arrogant. And impatient with people who didn't agree 100 percent with him on every idea. Usually, though, he kept his emotions under control. He'd tell you in that stone cold, unemotional voice that he thought you were being pigheaded. He practised that, keeping his emotions under control. He learned that lesson in medical school."

"Really?"

Dr. Matt swirled the ice around in his glass. "Oh, yes. This is something even little Sandi doesn't know. She thought her father walked on water. What she doesn't know is that he had a brief liaison with a woman while in college. She meant nothing to him, but she did have, shall we say, some womanly charms. She exuded sexiness. The aroma was thick as a fog around her. The affair was brief but produced a son, which Wes never knew about."

"He didn't? So what happened and how did you know about it?"

"Wes and I had been friends since college. I saw the girl a couple of times. Best friends don't have secrets from one another. I knew her name. Before she left for…California, I think it was…gosh, it was a long time ago since I've seen or even spoken with her. She didn't want to tie Wes down, but she wanted to keep the baby. She was exited. About two weeks later, I tried the number she gave me but it had been disconnected."

"What did Wes think of her leaving?"

"Surprisingly, he didn't seem too concerned about her. He said very little. Perhaps the relationship had fizzled to an end."

"Ever heard from her again?"

"No. I don't know what happened to her. Such a story might be distressing to Sandi. He clearly adored her, he was proud to have William following in his footsteps and he delighted in his grandchildren." Dr. Matt frowned and swirled the drink around some more. "Wes was a complicated man. He clearly had many gifts and a dedication to his patients. He wasn't the plaster saint Sandi thinks he was, and he had many good points, but like every man, he had flaws too. He made mistakes. But with one or two exceptions, I guess the scale weighed pretty heavily in his favor."

"Is it true that he'd been having headaches for the last several months of his life?" Dr. Matt nodded. "Wes complained of them to me. I suggested he go in for some tests. He said he would but he was always too busy. He never came in. I tended to doubt the headaches were anything more than the result of stress and his hard-driving schedule. But the fall downstairs could have triggered something fatal in the brain besides the obvious concussion that killed him. I'm not even sure they did an autopsy because the cause of death was obvious."

"Don't take this the wrong way, Matt, but where were you when Wes died?" Harry asked.

Dr. Matt didn't look offended. He smiled and even chuckled, then took another sip of his drink. "Yes, you have to ask such questions, don't you? As it turns out I don't have an alibi. I was home alone after leaving a social event. I find such parties boring. I left early and was reading when our esteemed hero slipped off this mortal coil. However, I was his doctor for more than two decades. If I wanted to kill him I could have found better ways than tossing him down the stairs and could have killed him sooner too. Before he married Maggie, for example."

Burnside swallowed his drink and set his glass back on the table. "Hope you have a good game, Matt. Does look like your slice is improving."

Chapter 7

Elm Grove, Nevada

Eight Weeks Later

Harry drove slowly back to his office and stopped at the Sugarloaf Café, a place in Elm Grove where he frequently went to unwind. Traffic was light. The snow had mostly been cleared by plows and the higher temperatures had eliminated much of the remainder. He was earning his pay, he supposed, but he hadn't uncovered much evidence. Not that he'd really expected to.

He had trouble believing that his one time father-in-law, Dr. Wesley Hunter had been murdered. He thought as he sipped his first beer. There was no trace of entry in the Hunter mansion. Which meant that the doctor had been alone with the housekeeper. But the housekeeper was in her fifties, probably mid-fifties if not closer to sixty. She threw the doctor down the stairs? Hardly likely. Besides, what was her motive? Could anyone else have entered the house? It was possible. Very remotely possible but not likely.

Snow had begun falling about two o'clock in the morning on the night Dr. Wes had died. So in theory, the killer could have slipped into the house and out again without leaving footprints in the snow. Still, Burnside thought there was opportunity. Dr. Hunter had a large mansion with only one servant, who had been in another part of the house. There had been an opportunity for someone to slip in. He would need to talk to the housekeeper. Harry's phone rang. He reached for it and. The voice seemed slightly familiar.

"Harry Burnside?"

"None other. Accept no substitutes."

"Harry, this is Brad Upton, FBI, remember me?" Harry shook and stared at the phone. Upton was one of the agents he had met on a previous case.

"Yes, yes…of course."

"I understand you're re-checking the death of Dr. Wes Hunter."

"I am."

"I have something to tell you. It may or may not have any relevance to your case but I'd thought you'd like to know. I don't want to speak over the phone."

"That's fine. Are you in Elm Grove?"

"I am. The FBI doesn't have a regular office here but we're in a little makeshift place."

Harry frowned. The FBI had to be in Elm Grove because of Dr. Wes's death. But why? Something beneath the surface, obviously. "I'm at the Sugarloaf Café."

"I can drop by. Be there in a few minutes."

Harry stayed silent for a few moments. This was a new twist on the case. He reached into his pocket and brought out a long, thin cigar. As he lit it, he noticed Upton coming in the door. The FBI man smiled and sat across the table from him. "So you have some information on the Hunter case?"

Upton nodded. "I have information. To be honest, I don't know if it is connected with Dr. Hunter or not. It's... an odd coincidence, if it is a coincidence." Harry leaned back and blew out a puff of gray smoke.

"Let's hear it."

"Two weeks ago, there was an security alert at the FBI and at the Department of Homeland Security. There's a terrorist leader known as Akhar Alwaki. He has a merry little band of murderers that is linked to al-Qaida. His right hand man is known as the Badger. The Badger, like his boss, has killed any number of people and is high on our 'wanted' list. We caught wind of a rumor that the Badger was in the area."

"In this area?" Harry asked in disbelief, lifting the cigar from his lips.

"Yes, we didn't think it was possible he had sneaked into the country but a number of agents were sent here, just in case. If the Badger was here, we had no idea what his mission was. Well anyway, we didn't spot him and we think the rumor was false. About 100 percent of rumors are, but we had to stay on alert."

Harry nodded. "But how does this relate to the Hunter case?"

"Because one of our agents, James Lontrell, has insomnia. He woke up one morning very early, about five in the morning, and couldn't get back to sleep. He tossed and turned, finally got up, and drove to a fast food place to

63

get breakfast and coffee. He went in the drive-through lane then turned his truck into the parking lot where he munched his sausage biscuit and drank his coffee.. In the distance, two men were walking. One had a dog, a Jack Russell terrier. That made Mr. Lontrell suspicious. Three years ago, Lontrell had investigated a contract killing. There'd been no arrests made, but one person of interest was a man named Oliver Townsend. Townsend looks like an average, middle-aged man - barrel-chested and balding but friendly and talkative. He's married and, from what we can tell, has few friends. But he does have a Jack Russell terrier."

Harry removed his cigar again, very slowly. He tapped the ash into an orange, seashell ashtray. "Go on," he said.

"Yes. At first, Lontrell shrugged it off and said it wasn't possible that Townsend had popped up again. He didn't get a close look at the man. The park was large, the two men didn't get close to Lontrell's car, and he didn't have any binoculars. But he watched them for a few minutes and then saw Townsend, or whoever it was, take his Jack Russell and get into a car and drive away. It was a cold day and the two men were bundled up. The man he believes was Townsend wore a hat and his jacket collar was turned up against the cold. So he can't be certain it was him."

"And Townsend is a hired killer?"

"If he is, he is a very, very careful one. He was a person of interest in that one case three years ago and although we suspect he's a professional assassin, we have no proof. None whatsoever. His advantage, or one of his advantages, is that he looks so ordinary that no one would suspect him. If we are correct in our suspicions..."

"What would a professional killer be doing in this city? When was he spotted?"

"The day after Dr. Hunter died."

Harry laid his cigar on the ashtray. He leaned forward, elbows on the table. "So a professional killer pops up the day after Dr. Wes Hunter died. That does put a new light on this case."

"But I must caution you. Lontrell suspected that he spied Townsend but he couldn't make a positive identification. If he was on the witness stand and asked by an attorney whether he was sure it was Townsend, he'd have to reply in the negative. It could have been someone else."

" But it might have been Townsend?"

"It might have been."

"And if Townsend was walking with someone, that someone might be his...employer?"

Upton nodded. "That was my thought. But if it was Townsend...well, no one else to my knowledge died during the couple of days before he was spotted. But again, there's no proof."

"Did your agent know who the second man was?"

"No, he was too far away. All Upton could tell us was that the second man looked younger. And that he was taller than Townsend."

Harry tapped the desk with his fingers. "Interesting. A lot of 'ifs' and a lot of 'maybes.' But very interesting." He looked at Upton. "Is that the only reason you're here?"

"Well, we had been keeping in touch with Dr. Wes and Hunter Company officials due to an bombing they had at the Idaho fields."

"I read about that. Find the culprit?"

Upton shook his head. "Not yet but we have some good leads. Evidence points to some radical environmentalists. We think maybe a couple of them got too radical. The pair we're looking at now were expelled from their environmental organization. They kept urging violence and the others said no."

"If they tried bombing, would they try murder?"

"You have to leave that option open, but right now I doubt it."

"Or would they hire it out? Mr. Townsend was seen in the area."

"Yes, that's true, and a possibility we are considering. But again, they seem to have a preference for explosives." Upton stood up suddenly and began to walk away. "I'll be in touch Harry," he said.

"Keep me posted." Harry replied.

Chapter 8

Elm Grove, Nevada

"Can I fix you anything else?" Marian asked, placing the steaming hot bowl of soup in front of Sandi.

"No, just soup is fine. Thank you, Marian." Sandi had moved into the Hunter mansion after her father's death because her stepmother had asked her to. Hinkley, for her part, had chosen to continue with her housekeeping duties. The housekeeper was a brown-haired woman, with high cheekbones, a small mouth and, Sandi thought, gentle eyes. There was always a kindness in her gaze. Hinkley looked toward a tall, brown recliner and edged over as if to sit down. Sandi's voice stopped her. "Can you stay for a minute?"

"Yes, Miss Sandi."

"Let's don't stand on formalities. Please sit down." The housekeeper looked uncomfortable but fidgeted into a dining chair. "Marian, I wanted to tell you that I'm not completely satisfied with the police investigation of my father's death. I've hired a private detective – my ex-husband, in fact – to help me but I want to do my own investigation too. So he may want to ask you some questions during his investigation."

"But Miss Sandi, shouldn't you let the police handle this? I know he was your father and you want to do everything possible, but the police are professionals."

"Even professionals need a little help now and then," Sandi said.

Marian sighed and settled back in the chair. "Your father was very kind to me and an excellent employer, so anything I can do to help, I will."

"Thank you. I did want to ask whether anything unusual happened the night of his death?"

Marian shook her head. "No ma'am. It was just another routine night. Your father came in about…six, I believe. I fixed him his dinner – beef tips with gravy on potatoes, with vegetables. He laughed and joked with me, as he usually did. Your father was always a very busy man but he never seemed too busy to talk. I mean, he was never rushing off to do something or yelling or agitated. He was casual and always greeted me and even talked with me. That night I remembered that he even asked how my son was doing. My son works for him, you know?"

"Really? I didn't know that. What does he do?"

"He's an engineer. Currently, he is in Elm Grove at the headquarters of Dr. Wes's petroleum company."

"In Granite Tech?"

"Yes, ma'am. He's done fieldwork and was in petroleum when he was transferred down here about eight months ago. I'm very proud of my son. His name is Steven. He was one of the scientists who helped discover the techniques the company uses for fracking. Well, I think he improved them rather than discover them."

Sandi stared at her, puzzled. "Steven? Steven Gifford?"

"Yes, Gifford is his father's last name."

"I never realized Steven was your son."

"Yes, he's my only child and he's a very good man. I believe he inherits his intelligence from his father – his father (now passed away; may he rest in peace), also knew mechanics."

"Must be a comfort having him nearby," Sandi said quietly.

Marian's eyes filled with tears. "Yes, it is. It's wonderful. I was so happy when he was transferred." She shook herself and waved her hand as if dismissing her words. "Oh, I'm sorry. I started talking about my son and got off the subject. But after your father had dinner, he went into his study. I brought him his usual cup of Irish coffee at about eight o'clock and asked if he wanted anything. He didn't; he was going to take some of the evening to read. Said that he wanted to think about a few business matters and that he could think best in his study, with peace and quiet around. About an hour later I checked on him once again. He said he was fine and wouldn't be needing anything else, so I could go to bed. And I did. About an hour later, I was asleep."

Sandi frowned. Her fingers scratched her jaw. "So you were asleep when Dad slipped or…well, when he fell on the stairs."

"Yes, ma'am."

"You didn't hear anything?"

69

"No, I'm sorry. He did mumble something when I checked him the second time. I didn't fully understand what he said."

Could it have been a word or name he was trying to say? Think, Marian. This could be important," insisted Sandi.

I think it sounded like…Eve. But I'm not sure. If I'd heard, I could have called the EMTs. Maybe it would've saved your father's life." She shook her head. "But I heard nothing. I didn't wake up until the next morning." Sandi looked at Marian quizzically.

"It's not your fault, Marian. Did you happen to hear anything before Dad fell. Anything between the time you left Dad and the time you went to bed?"

The housekeeper shook her head again. "No ma'am. My room is some ways from both the stairs and the study. There was no sound to disturb my sleeping." Sandi swallowed a spoonful of the soup.

"That's very good. Thank you, Marian."

Thirty minutes after Sandi Burnside left, Marian Hinkley responded to a tap on the back door. She opened it and smiled when she saw Gifford. "Come in," she said.

* * *

Her son was a solid, well-built man in his forties. Six-two, he had broad shoulders and a crooked smile that would have appeared odd and perhaps disconcerting if he didn't beam with friendliness. Steven Gifford had an optimistic outlook even when circumstances did their best to make situations appear pessimistic. He took off his coat and kissed his mother on her cheek.

"I've just made some coffee. Would you like some?"

"Yes, it's still a bit chilly out there. Better than it was but weather for shorts yet." She poured him a cup as he sat down at the kitchen table.

"Sandi Burnside was just here." Steven's coffee cup stopped halfway to his mouth. He raised his eyebrows, then sipped the coffee.

"What did she want?"

"To question me. To ask about the night her father died."

"What did you tell her?"

"Nothing. I knew nothing. I was sleeping. But I imagine she's suspicious."

"Mother, why should she be suspicious of you? Does she think a woman actually pushed threw Dr. Hunter down the stairs? He was in his sixties, but he was in good shape. Didn't you tell me he went to the gym three times a week?"

She nodded. "He did. And ate well. He believed in good nutrition. I don't think he was sick a day in his life."

"So it's doubtful that a much smaller woman – also in her sixties – could throw him down a staircase," Steven said.

"Still, I think she is suspicious. I was the only one in the house with him. Doesn't that make me a suspect?"

"Not necessarily. Besides, wasn't the fall an accident? Didn't the police establish that?"

"Not everyone is satisfied with that conclusion," his mother said. "Perhaps if I was his daughter, I wouldn't be satisfied either."

71

Steven sipped his coffee again. "It does seem a bit incongruous. The great, influential Dr. Wesley Hunter, whose shadow is over cast three states if not more, who has made his name in both medicine and business, slips on a staircase and kills himself. His admirers say he was a giant of a man, so the end doesn't fit his life. But accidents happen, to even great men.

She nodded. "I suppose so."

He leaned back in the chair. "Now that the doctor is dead, would you like to retire and come to stay with me? I have a big house here. You adore Jenna and she loves you." Steven smiled. "You can have the west wing of the house all to yourself. Plenty of room and a great cable system."

"Yes, there's nothing for me here now. Perhaps it is time to retire." She gave a sardonic smile. "I could take up golf."

"Or any number of other hobbies."

"Yes, as soon as Mrs. Hunter decides what she wants to do with the house, I'll retire."

"Good." Steven stood up and grabbed his jacket. He looked at his mother. "Did the doctor ever realize—"

His mother shook her head. "No, he never did."

Chapter 9

Sandi Burnside was sitting at the Sugarloaf chewing on a chocolate glaze when Harry ambled in. He gave her a wide smile. She returned it and waved him to the table. He paused to buy two multi-colored glaze donuts before coming over and sitting down. "Are you on a diet?" she asked, as he bit into the pink and white frosting.

"A diet?"

"A donut diet?"

"Yes, these are the best kind."

"So how do you lose weight on that diet?"

He shrugged. "Who said anything about losing weight?" She laughed. His manner reminded her of why she'd married him.

"Anyway, you wanted to share some info with me."

He nodded. As he munched, he told her Brad Upton's story about the possible, if mysterious, hit-man named Oliver Townsend. He mentioned also that Mr. Townsend had possibly been seen in Elm Grove two days after the death of her father. For a minute, Sandi said nothing. Then

73

she eased forward in her seat. "If that's true, it's an amazing coincidence."

"Yes, it is. If true."

Sandi tapped her lips with a finger. "So, Harry, could you get your FBI piles to do some investigating? Maybe check to see if there are any credit card receipts from Mr. Townsend from the local area. Could they dig a little and find out where he was on the day of Dad's death?"

"I should have thought of that when Brad came to the office. It may take some arm-twisting."

"You have a good hammerlock. Twist their arms." Harry finished the last of his first donut, then sipped his Coke.

"How can you drink that with donuts?" Sandi asked.

"Very easily," he answered.

She shook her head. "Anyway, can you get the FBI to dig a little deeper?"

"Maybe. The agents were here on another case, which turned out to be just a rumor. But I do have a few favors I might be able to call in."

"Good. Can you get a picture of Townsend?"

"Yes, I should be able to swing that."

"Get two. One for me, so that I can take it to local shops and ask if they recognize him."

"That's a long shot. Know how many shops and businesses there are in Elm Grove?"

"Ninety-eight percent of reporting and ninety-eight percent of detective work is legwork. You pound the pavements. Out of a hundred people who haven't seen the guy, you might get one who says "Yes, I saw that guy last week.""

"And you might get all hundred people saying no, I haven't seen him."

"It's worth a shot."

"Okay, when I get it, I'll email it to you."

"Anything known about the man Townsend was allegedly with?"

Harry shook his head. "Not a thing. He was described as being younger, maybe, and taller."

"Not much to go on."

"Not really."

Sandi watched as her ex-husband bit into his second donut. "Still, it's something. It sure is curious that an alleged hit-man might have been in the area during the time that Dad died." Even though they were discussing a serious subject, Sandi couldn't help but flinch when Burnside took another gulp of his Coke after swallowing another hunk of donut. "Harry, what type of diet are you on again?"

"The Coke and donut diet. It's for those people who have no willpower." She didn't know whether to laugh or flinch again. He wiped his mouth with a blue napkin.

"Yes, it is odd but as yet, we have nothing to tie the alleged – and I stress alleged – hit-man to the death of your father."

"Did anyone else drop dead in the city about that time?"

"I don't know. I'll check the obituary list. But I don't think there were any murders during that time. By the way, your father didn't have any skeletons in his closet, did he?" The words pushed her hard against the chair.

"No, of course not. Why would you ask that?"

"Just wondering. It's the type of question private investigators ask. Most people – even some very good people – have things in their past that they're not proud of. Perhaps even things they keep from their daughters."

"I'm not aware of anything," Sandi said quickly, a touch of indignation in her voice. Then she switched the subject. "So how long before you can get a picture of Townsend?"

"Brad's dependable and usually very quick. I should be able to send you it tomorrow."

"Good. I won't rush you." She inclined her head and left.

Chapter 10

Summerlin, Nevada

The last thing Dr. William Hunter wanted was to meet with environmental activists. He had things to do. There was nothing pressing, but as an administrator there was always paperwork galore and personnel matters to deal with. For that matter, he had golf to play. He didn't want to waste his time and words on anti-fracking eco-freaks. But he had agreed to talk with them. It would be the last time. He smiled as Steven Gifford came into the conference room. "Dr. Hunter, how are you?"

"Cranky and grouchy. How are you, Steve?"

"Doing well."

"I still don't know how you talked me into this. The meeting will be a waste of time."

"Possibly. But it's also feasible that we can talk some common sense into the protestors. I think – and I know you agree with me – that their position is not based on science but on ideology. If we can show by facts and figures…"

"They won't listen." Hunter sighed. "You could establish that fracking cures cancer and they still wouldn't like it. It's a religion to them and they'll stay religious no matter what science says."

"I am more optimistic than you."

"Perhaps I'm just more realistic," Hunter said.

When the three activists came in, both Hunter and Gifford shook their hands and greeted them warmly. One was an older gentleman and the other two were young. They looked like college students, Hunter thought. The older man was thin, balding on top with an oval face. Despite the lack of hair, he still managed to sport a slender, gray ponytail behind his neck. He identified himself as Dr. Auri Goslen, although he didn't say what field the degree was in. The young man was blond, a bit stout and had a chubby face. Deep-set brown eyes below a forehead that was slightly too big. The girl was a wide-eyed brunette with a vivacious smile and a pleasant voice. They were invited to sit down and, after exchanging a few pleasantries, Dr. Hunter told them to proceed with their presentation, although he warned them that he had probably heard everything before. And he had.

The doctor had brought a few maps and charts with him and the two younger individuals helped him set them up. He lifted a pointer from his coat, stretched it out and pointed to a multi-colored chart. Hunter sighed but decided not to interrupt. The good doctor seemed so diligent and dedicated. Let him ramble on and get it out of his system, Hunter thought. His mind wandered as the man rattled off facts and figures, most of which Hunter knew to be inaccurate.

Gifford was more involved. He asked a few questions, which were promptly answered. Twice he asked follow-up questions, pinpointing a weakness in the presentation. While

Gifford was in discussing with the three, Hunter wondered whether anyone would notice if he closed his eyes. They'd probably pick up on that and consider it disrespectful. He looked toward his younger colleague and decided the man was not only an excellent engineer but had the capacity to suffer fools lightly, a talent he had never picked up. Gifford's voice was firm but polite and his eyes alert with interest, as he engaged the three environmentalists. He seemed to be having a good time.

Dr. Hunter wondered if they could conclude the meeting soon so he could get in nine holes before darkness would make golf impossible. Maybe not, if the other doctor kept talking. He was probably a college professor. So many of them rambled on forever and had no idea what they were talking about. Dr. Goslen seemed to be winding down, and Hunter started to perk up. He snapped the pointer closed. "So you see why we are so concerned about fracking. We fear the environmental consequences will be catastrophic," Goslen said. He shifted on his feet, and a small sigh escaped him as he sat down at the table.

"Yes, just had arson at our Idaho facility," said Hunter. "I'm guessing the arsonist or arsonists felt the same way you do."

"We condemn violence," said Goslen. "All violence. Besides we are not in Idaho." Goslen shook his head vigorously and continued. "We believe in peaceful protests and civic action. We don't carry guns or bombs."

Dr. Hunter nodded, non-verbally telling Steven to do the rebuttal. Gifford didn't stand, but placed his elbows on the table, then opened his hands in a gesture of reconciliation. "I deeply appreciate your concern. Despite stereotypes, oil

79

men value the environmental too. We live and work in the outdoors and often prefer rural areas to cities. We certainly don't want to destroy what we love. However, I must say that most of the so-called facts you presented are not accurate. With all due respect, you have been viewing too many Hollywood films. The one that comes to mind is the anti-fracking movie. Where residents of a small town turned the faucet of the kitchen sink, and flames came out. Things like that. It doesn't work like that in real life. Earthquakes are not more prevalent in areas where fracking is taking place and the scientific data proves this."

He raised his hand when the three started to protest. "Please, you were allowed to give your presentation. Let me present the rebuttal. The opposition to fracking is not based on science or knowledge or facts. It is based on ideology. A small number of people do not like our nation being dependent on oil or what they call a carbon-based economy. But solar, biofuels or wind power don't have the capability, as yet, to sustain a national economy. The current administration in Washington has invested taxpayers' money into many sun-based or wind turbine companies and most of them have gone bankrupt."

When the three started to object again, he nodded and quickly said, "No, not all of them, but many have. And they went bankrupt with taxpayers' money. Taxpayers got penalized in taxes. If the federal investors had bothered to look at the facts – both scientific and financial – they would never have invested. I certainly don't think any of those federal bureaucrats invested their own money in such projects. No doubt they put their own funds into a bank to collect interest or invested it in safe projects that will guarantee a return. I could give you statistic after statistic and spend hours providing scientific data but instead I will give you these folders that support my scientific arguments."

From a drawer, he pulled out three blue folders and passed them over. The two younger individuals opened the covers and skimmed through the pages. "You should also realize that in March of 2013, for the first time, the United States produced more oil than Saudi Arabia. Although little noticed, it was a pivotal point in our history. The more oil we produce, the less we have to depend on regimes that have supported terrorism. It also means we are not dependent on foreign nations for our energy needs. "Our production of shale oil, through fracking, is one of the main reasons for this triumph. The nation could not have reached that landmark without the significant increases in shale oil production in North Dakota and Texas.

The rise of the US to become the world's largest petroleum producer is another important milestone in America's new era of energy abundance, and reflects the importance of the breakthrough. Revolutionary extraction technologies (hydraulic fracturing and horizontal drilling) have brought a true shale energy revolution to this land. And that's not even considering the enormous economic benefits that fracking provides to a struggling economy. Our unemployment rate is high and millions of people are underemployed in low-paying jobs because there's nothing else for them. Fracking improves wages and provides a high-quality life for thousands – tens of thousands – of people.

And it also has a ripple effect. Fracking is providing quality jobs for tens of thousands of people. So why don't you read my folder and we can schedule another meeting?"

The three nodded and, to Hunter's surprise, did not look as angry or as agitated as he thought they might. They were very pleasant as they left the conference room. Gifford shook hands with all three and walked with them to the door. The older man and the woman had already left the room when he clasped the hand of the younger man and said, "Sorry, I don't think I heard your name."

"Thomas Valdane," the man said. "You gave a very effective rebuttal."

"Thank you."

Valdane looked around and waited until his two friends were completely out of earshot. "You play a very good role, Steven. I almost believed everything you said."

Gifford smiled. "Sometimes it helps being a good actor. So did your people have anything to do with that little Idaho incident?"

Valdane slapped Gifford on the shoulder. "Sometimes it's best to say nothing, old friend."

Chapter 11

Elm Grove, Nevada

Three Months Later

When Sandi's phone rang at six o'clock that evening, she looked at the caller ID. "Hello, Harry," she answered, charmingly.

"I just emailed you a photo of Oliver Townsend. It's a pretty good one. Headshot, but it shows him clear. No blurred edges."

"Thanks. I see you were very effective with your FBI buddies. What else have they dug up?"

"Let's just say that we exchange favors from time to time and they owed me one. When they want something done, the Feds can move fast. Of course, they get overtime."

Sandi laughed. "Ah, but they're giving us good service for our money, at least in this case."

"I have two other pieces of news for you too. One is good, the other is bad, or at least neutral."

"You're beginning to alarm me. Let's go with neutral first. Perhaps we should do this in person."

"Meet me at the Le Paris in thirty minutes."

Harry Burnside sat slouched on a barstool, happily sipping his favorite beverage. Harry was the establishment's only customer at that time of day, unless you counted the slip of a woman in a tight, see-through blouse who sat silently in the corner. Harry wasn't immediately aware of Sandi hurrying through the swing doors and seating herself on the stool next to his. And when he did see her, and was about to kiss her on the cheek, she put her hand up. "Look who just came through those doors." Both heads turned in time to witness two neatly dressed young ladies, both hanging on tightly to Sandi's brother, Dr. Bill Hunter. Sandi watched unbelievingly as he walked past without any acknowledgement of their presence. Sandi and Harry looked at each other in surprise.

Harry spoke in an undertone. "Townsend is suspected in two killings and the agency figures he's probably been involved in others as well. The bad news is his choice of weapon – a small caliber handgun, a .32 or even a .22. The guns he allegedly used have never been found. He's a very careful man."

Sandi chewed on her lip. "Close in. That indicates he likes to be very near the victim."

"Yes, but he uses guns. He's never been known to break a guy's neck. And he doesn't look that strong. Of course, below that pudginess may lay an arm of steel. But your father was in good condition. I wonder if Townsend could have pushed him down the stairs. In a fight, Townsend might have been the guy flying to the floor."

"Possibly, but if he could have gotten the upper hand on dad, or come up behind him or something like that, he could have pulled it off."

"But why would he? If he was that close, he could have pulled out his trusty sidearm."

"Yes, that is puzzling."

"Again, this is only if Townsend was involved. There's no evidence of that yet, but then there's no evidence tying him to the other murders he's suspected of either."

"So what's the good news?"

"After considerable conversation and a little arm-pulling, I did get our distinguished federal agency to do a little checking on Mr. Townsend. It seems that the eagle-eyed agent was correct. Mr. Townsend was in the area. The pudgy little guy spotted in the park was probably him. Credit records show that an Oliver Townsend used a credit card to purchase two coffees at the local Starbucks two days before your father died." Sandi waited a moment to respond. She breathed deeply before replying.

"So if he wasn't in the area to kill Dad, what else was he doing here?"

"Passing through? Oddly enough there's no credit card for a motel. Just one for the coffees and one for dinner that night at a local steak joint. Other than that, he must have paid cash."

"Wait a minute. He paid for two coffees?"

"Yes. That's what it said on the bill."

"Starbucks usually gives you a large cup. He wouldn't need two coffees. Was he buying for someone else as well?"

"Might have been. That thought had occurred to me."

"I'll make inquiries."

"Be careful. This is a hit-man we are talking about." Her finger tapped her lips again.

"I'll be careful. But this is just too pat. A hit man—"

"Alleged hit-man."

"An alleged hit man is in the area for a few days. During one of those days my father dies. I loved Dad and I think he was a good man, but famous men and rich men have enemies. So maybe there was someone who came out of the woodwork, someone who hated Dad. Someone who could have hired Townsend." She shook her head. "By the way, where does Townsend live?"

Harry drew back. "You're not going to see him, are you?"

"I might. Drop by and ask him a few questions."

"How would that conversation go, Sandi. 'Oh, by the way, could you tell me if you killed my father and also reveal who hired you?'"

Sandi shrugged as she watched Harry chew on some almonds and pretzels. "Maybe I can catch him in a talkative mood."

Harry groaned. "I don't think Townsend is ever in a talkative mood. Besides, I don't know where he lives."

"Could you talk to your FBI buddies? They would know."

"Sandi, I don't think he's going to confess to you. You can be very persuasive but I think even your charm wouldn't be enough to get a hit-man to talk about his crimes. You should let me handle him."

Sandi through up her hands. "Sometimes you could be so stubborn. I need to know who killed my father. I'm not going to rest until I bring this person to justice. Try to understand, Harry. I must know. I must. Can you get me his address?"

Harry swallowed. "I'll send it to you. But I'll make the trip and talk to him. Dr. Wes was our children's grandfather, remember. And I do know how you must be hurting. But this is the last favor I can call in with the FBI."

Chapter 12

When Maggie Hunter left the coiffure on Missouri Avenue that morning, she was counting on not getting married again or even seeing Dr. Ross. Yet she found herself turning into the parking lot of his office. She eased down into an amply-cushioned, burgundy chair in Dr. Matthew Ross's study. He walked over and kissed her cheek before sitting in an adjacent chair.

"I was very sorry to hear about Wes's death. It was a tragedy."

She gave a flash-of-a-switchblade smile. "Spare me the sentimentalities, Matt." She shrugged.

"It seemed like the thing to say."

"At the funeral, maybe. Not when we're alone," she said. "Besides, considering our other rendezvous, I don't think many people would believe it, especially his family." Dr. Matt frowned. His lover was more cold-blooded than he was. Although he loved Maggie, he did regret his friend's passing. Perhaps he should change the subject.

"I thought the service was very moving and appropriate. Wes was a true Methodist." He smiled. "Did I tell you his reaction to that line in the movie, The Story of Jackie Robinson.

"No."

"We went to a screening. Branch Rickey was a staunch Methodist. He thought it was God's will that he integrate baseball with other major American sports. In one line in the movie, he says, "I'm a Methodist. Jackie is a Methodist. God is a Methodist." Wes loved the line." Maggie smiled faintly. Since Wes's death three month's ago now, Maggie had seemed depressed, withdrawn even, which was not like her at all. Ross studied the woman he'd loved for so long. She was five-seven, with beautiful brown hair and gray, distinct eyes. Flawless skin. Small mouth but when the lips smiled, his heart skipped a beat. It was a mystery to him how one woman should have such an emotional hold over him. He couldn't really define it. Not in terms of beauty or personality or even physical attraction. No woman had captured his heart in the way that Maggie Hunter had. Try as he might, he couldn't break free from those invisible bonds.

"Perhaps we should 't even be seen together until some time has passed." Pink lipstick covered her pale lips. The voice was matter-of-fact.

"We're old friends and I'm still the family physician, unless you want to change that. Our meeting shouldn't arouse suspicions. We're two old friends comforting one another."

"But we were comforting one another before Wes passed," she said, a sardonic tone crept into her voice. Her comment made him uncomfortable. He would have preferred not talking about their affair. At least not today. He rose from his chair.

"Can I get you something to drink? Tea? Coffee? Lemonade?

"Lemonade, thank you." He walked to the bar and instead poured a French red wine into two glasses. He knew that she loathed lemonade. He offered one to Maggie.

"So what exactly did happen to Wes?" she asked.

He winced and drank a sip from the glass. "He fell down the stairs, Maggie. Hit his head and it caused a concussion. It must have happened sometime during the night. Wes often stayed up late, studying or reading. Sometime between ten or clock and six – which is when the housekeeper found him – he simply stumbled and fell."

"Doesn't seem like Wes would die that way," she said.

"Life and death don't always go the way we plan. Wes wasn't getting any younger, after all. Even great men get old. Even great men can stumble and fall." Maggie kept looking at him with her gray eyes. The voice wasn't accusatory but factual.

"You didn't kill him, did you, Matt?"

He had half expected the question so he didn't become indignant. He just turned and looked directly at her. "No, Maggie, I did not."

"Sorry. But it's a question that Harry Burnside would ask if he knew our arrangement. You hear Sandi hired him to investigate?"

"Harry? Her ex-husband? Yes. I forgot. Bill had mentioned it. If I'd wanted to kill Wes, it would have been before your wedding to him, not after."

"But if you had, would you tell me?"

"Yes, Maggie, I wouldn't lie to you. Even if I tried, you could see through the lie."

Maggie looked at him in surprise. But could I? she thought. I can't go on like this. I have to do something.

Chapter 13

Sandi Burnside took a look at the photo of alleged hit-man Oliver Townsend. He certainly didn't look like a godfather. The camera or cellphone or whatever else had taken the picture had photographed him when he was smiling. Slightly large lips for his face, she thought, but the man did have a nice smile. Bright, even teeth. Nose slightly large, but not prominently so. The round, gold spectacles on the blue eyes gave him almost a scholarly look. He certainly didn't look menacing, she thought. Of course, hit-men don't want to look menacing or distinguished. They don't want to stand out in a crowd. They don't want to be remembered. It's the same with spies. In films, spies are dashing, handsome and memorable. In reality, they don't want to be noticed when they walk into a building or a defence complex. They want to fade into the woodwork. All killers do.

Mr. Townsend, Sandi decided, would not be out of place in the local Kroger picking up a bag of carrots and two pounds of ground beef. Other shoppers wouldn't look twice at him. She put the photo into her purse as she opened the door and stepped into the Starbucks parking lot. Another storm was predicted but she put her foot down onto snowless asphalt. The wintery results of the last storm had been cleared away. Even so, the air remained cold. Sandi wore a heavy jacket as she walked into the store. She waited until she saw a waitress she knew, cleaning tables.

She walked over to her. "Molly, may I talk to you for a few seconds?" The waitress stopped wiping the small black table. When she recognized Sandi, she gave a broad smile; the broadcaster always tipped well.

"Sandi, hello! Sure I've got a minute. You're a good customer – the boss won't mind if I chat with you." They sat down at the table and Sandi removed the photograph from her purse, along with a fifty-dollar bill. She offered both items to the waitress.

"Molly, this is fifty dollars for your time. I want you to look carefully and tell me if you've ever seen this man. About a week ago, he was in here. I know because his credit card shows a purchase here."

Molly took the photograph and studied it. There was no hint of recognition on her face. Eyes were blank. Lips didn't move. "Why do you want to know about this man?"

"Let's just say he might be involved in a matter that I want to question him about. He bought two coffees and I suspect he might have had someone else with him. Molly pocketed the money. She looked at the photograph for a minute, then shook her head.

"Can't say I've seen him. I see so many people who pass through here. If he came in, he can't have been very memorable." She raised her head and looked at Sandi. "Can you stick around for a few minutes? It's a slow time now. I can ask the other girls."

"Thank you. I appreciate that. There's another fifty if someone recognizes him." Sandi popped the photo with a fingernail.

"That might help. Can I get you something while you're waiting?" Molly asked.

"Low-cal latte."

There was a sudden flurry of additional activity at the far side of the café. Sandi looked briefly for any recognizable faces, but they were mainly office personnel. She reached for her phone to check any missed calls. There weren't any calls.

"One low-cal latte, Ma'am."

"Thank you." Sandi sipped the coffee while Nell passed the photo around. Sandi thought she really should make an effort to see her stepmother, now that the woman was back in town. The meeting wouldn't be effusive but she should say hello. Despite her dislike of Margaret Hunter, her dad seemed to have enjoyed the marriage and did not regret his choice. So if he was happy, Sandi told herself, I should be happy too. But she'd never hit it off with her stepmother. It was just a matter of chemistry. They had disliked each other at first sight. A second sight too. Like kerosene and matches, the two did not mix.

Sandi had never been sure just how much her stepmother loved her father. True, from what she knew about her father's trust and estate, Maggie benefitted little from her husband's death. If she had, Sandi would have seriously suspected her stepmother of hiring a hit-man. Maggie was also an environmentalist at heart and despised fracking. If she had control of her deceased husband's estate, she might put an end to the process, despite the fiscal losses she'd endure.

Wait a minute…Sandi's fingers tapped her coffee cup. She frowned. The bitter idea made her wince but resonated in her mind. What if some wacky eco-freak – say the local folks down the street at the Earth First office – didn't know about all the codicils in Wesley Hunter's will, did not know that the estate would be left to his children, and not to his second wife. Say one eco-freak knew of Maggie's sympathy to the movement. That wouldn't be difficult – Sandi's stepmother was hardly shy in supporting environmental causes. So what if the activist mistakenly believed that it would be Maggie who would control the Hunter oil interests in the event of Wes's death? That would be a motivation for murder. If some wacko believed he could stop some of the fracking going on by killing Dr. Wesley Hunter, wouldn't he do it? Certainly. Probably without hesitation.

But that didn't mean that her stepmother would have any knowledge of such a scenario. Still, in this section of the country amongst the environmental community, her father stood for fracking. His medical accomplishments were overlooked. He had been condemned as a greedy oil man who was destroying the Earth. Such rhetoric could prompt a mentally-unhinged man or woman to…And her stepmother was a friend of many environmentalists. She looked up as Molly returned to clear the dishes. "Thank you, Molly. That coffee was the best I've had in months."

Chapter 14

Banning, California

Five Months Later

Oliver Townsend enjoyed a warm climate, so he was quite content in Banning, California, a small city about 80 miles east of Los Angeles. He liked small cities too. Due to his occupation, he had to work in big cities from time to time and two of his jobs occurred in the huge city eighty miles to the west. He hated the traffic, the congestion, the crowds. Two other jobs mandated trips to New York City, a location he found as abhorrent as L.A. To him, it was unimaginable how people could live in such places. In Banning, there was ample room, plenty of open spaces, and streams and lakes where he could pursue his avid hobby of fishing. He found the fishing quite contemplative.

Being a hit-man required patience, a much overlooked virtue. Oliver had to monitor his subject and be aware of the man's movements (he had only once been asked to kill a woman). To do so took great perseverance, tenacity and patience. If you wanted to kill someone, it helped to know that they would be at a certain place at five o'clock without fail. The most difficult people to kill were those individuals who didn't have a routine.

He didn't mind sitting patiently in his small boat, line in the water, waiting for a fish to bite. In spite of his high-tension profession, he had the amazing psychological ability to keep calm and, for that matter, to doze off during the daytime. He never had trouble going to sleep at night. If everyone had his nervous system, the sales of Valium, Xanax and other tranquilizers would plummet and the drug companies would go bankrupt. He'd just checked his bank account online and smiled to himself to see that the latest payment for his services had been deposited. After transferring ten percent of the funds into his saving account, which now ran to medium-five figures, he returned to his comfortable recliner and flicked on the baseball channel. Several analysts were making their predictions for the upcoming season.

When he wasn't fishing, Townsend enjoyed watching baseball. He was not a native southern Californian but he rooted for the closest geographical teams – the Los Angeles Dodgers and the San Diego Chargers. Even before moving to Banning, he'd cheered for the Dodgers because, for several years in his childhood, he'd lived in Vero Beach, Florida which at that time had been the spring training home of the Dodgers. He'd attended several games as a child and even got an autograph from the great Orel Hershiser, perhaps the finest Dodger pitcher since Sandy Koufax. To this day, he remembered that Hershiser, although an exceptional pitcher, was exceedingly modest and friendly as he signed the autograph for the young fan. He was pleased to hear that the baseball pundits predicted the Dodgers had a very good chance of making the World Series during the coming season. The team's pitching was solid and the offence, if not spectacular, was better than average.

Townsend's wife was out of town, visiting her relatives in northern California. He had not planned to go with her because he didn't know how long his assignment in Elm City would last. As it was, he'd arrived back at home the day after she left. She was a plump, pleasant woman who adored him and who thankfully didn't ask any questions of his work. She believed he was a fiscal and stock market consultant who sometimes had to travel to meet with clients. The clang of the doorbell interrupted Oliver's nodding agreement with the baseball pundits.

Frowning, he hit the mute button and walked to the door. When he opened it, two gentlemen wearing dark glasses and dark blue suits stood in front of him. Both looked to be in their mid-thirties and both clearly spent much of their time in the gym. Broad chests, piercing eyes, and – to Townsend – disturbing smiles. The taller man had light brown hair. The other man's was dark brown. Both had the disturbing smiles. As if they knew something he didn't. "Mr. Oliver Townsend?" the darker man said.

"Yes." They both showed him official I.D. cards. The darker man was Calvin Hadley. The tall guy, Terry Denton. Townsend took one identification card and held it up, then handed it back to the agent.

"I wasn't aware that your agency was allowed to operate inside the United States," Townsend said.

"In special cases, we can."

99

"And is this a special case, Mr. Hadley?"

"It might be." Hadley's disturbing smile became even wider.

"Then by all means, come in. But I don't see how I could be of any help to agents of our nation's fine intelligence service." Townsend sat back in his chair as the two agents eased onto a burgundy sofa. "May I offer you a drink – a cup of coffee, maybe? I generally drink coffee through the day, so I always have a fresh pot brewing."

"No, thank you. We just had a late lunch at one of the charming little restaurants in town," replied Denton.

"So how can I help you?"

Hadley produced a picture from inside his jacket. He handed it to Townsend. "Could you tell us if you have ever seen his man?" The man in question was Arabic, with a thick mustache, olive-brown skin, and a scar on his forehead. Young, younger than 40.

Townsend thought. He shook his head. "No, why would I?"

There was a casual tone in Hadley's voice that made Townsend feel anything but relaxed. "We thought you might have bumped into him a short time ago. You both were in the same region. Up near Elm Grove. Not too far from here."

Townsend had developed a calm demeanor, and he didn't jolt or even flinch at Hadley's words. But his mouth was dry as he handed back the photograph "I believe I was up there some time ago, but I didn't see this man or anyone who looked like him. Who is he?"

"He's a terrorist," Hadley answered. "We put out a story that a well-known terrorist might be in the vicinity but that we'd checked it out and found it to be just a rumor. That was the official line. In fact, the rumor was completely true."

Townsend remained unshaken, but he did pause before speaking. "I don't work for terrorists and what would someone like that be doing around Elm Grove? Shouldn't they be in the Middle East overthrowing governments or scatter acid on girls walking to school?"

"You'd think so, wouldn't you? But terrorist groups have longer-term strategies too," Denton said.

Hadley looked at the photo now. He held it up in his hand. "This man goes by the nickname of 'The Badger'. He's a member of one of the groups affiliated with al-Qaida. A very skilled member of the group, very well acquainted with various method of killing people."

"I hope you caught him," Townsend said. "But you haven't told me what he was doing in this region. And I'm certain I've never seen this man. Nor would I associate with him." Townsend always kept his calm but Hadley looked relaxed too. Relaxed and confident.

Hadley leaned back on the sofa and crossed his legs. "I will tell you," he said. "His presence at Elm Grove may be related to those long-term strategies we mentioned. The terrorist groups and their supporters hope to gain control of all, or at least most, of the Middle East. And they've been successful to a degree. The new president of Egypt is a former member of the Muslim Brotherhood, which is extremely sympathetic to terrorists. Fights between moderates and extreme jihadists have taken place in Tunisia, Morocco, Syria, and Libya. Turkey is leaning their way too.

101

French troops, thank goodness, kicked the jihadists out of Mali, at least for the time being."

"But the Egyptian's president is having a tough time even feeding the population. The economy is crashing. That may give the citizens pause. Popular support for the Muslim Brotherhood is diminishing." Townsend added.

Hadley smiled. "Ah, I see you keep up with international news, Mr. Townsend."

"I try to stay informed," Townsend said.

Hadley looked at his partner. "That's always good. Always useful to have an intelligent, informed electorate, isn't it?"

"Sure is. It's a shame that more people are not as informed as Mr. Townsend is," said Denton. Townsend couldn't tell if there was sarcasm in the tone or not.

"What has not been in the news yet," said Hadley, "is that the jihadists want power on the world stage. If they take over the Middle East, they will wield that power only if the Arab nations keep their monopoly on oil. Oil has been a potent economic and political weapon for the past forty or fifty years. Without the oil, they're just a bunch of camel jockeys with third-rate nations and decaying economies."

Townsend looked at both his visitors anxiously. "And what does oil in the Middle East have to do with me?"

Hadley ignored the question and continued. "But recently with the enormous production of shale oil, government officials in Middle East nations have realized that their power is slipping away. That recognition has also occurred to the jihadists. Without oil, they have no power and shale oil will undercut production and prices of Middle

102

Eastern oil. Saudi Arabia and other nations like being on top and flush with money. Without the oil revenues they're on the bottom of the heap again. No one will care about them. Recently, the United States overtook Saudi Arabia in oil production. That was a red-letter day that will have future repercussions for both the United States and the Middle East."

"And exactly how does this concern Elm Grove?"

"I'm coming to that. Our agency, from time to time, carries out electronic and satellite anti-terrorist surveillance. We believe that these terrorists are considering attacks on shale oil companies, which would hinder or possibly prevent production. A few bombs strategically placed on pipelines or production sites could cripple the industry. We've also heard rumors that they've discussed killing several top ranking officials of shale oil companies. That's a short list but it would have included Dr. Wesley Hunter."

Townsend shrugged. "I still don't see where you're going."

"Dr. Wesley Hunter lived in Elm Grove and died during the time you were there. See where I'm going now? It's a one-way street leading to your house." Hadley paused for a moment. "So why were you in Elm Grove?"

Townsend shook his head. "I was passing through. I like to travel. I often take car trips. It was a nice little town so I stayed for a few days."

"Don't lie to us," Denton said. This time the voice was hard, like a steam hammer pummeling cement. "Our colleagues at the FBI have told us of your profession, Mr. Townsend. Not that we object. You tend to rid the nation of criminals and rather ruthless criminals at that. The human race is better off without them."

"I'm sure I don't know what you are talking about. Even the FBI can be mistaken."

"Not this time. As I said, Mr. Townsend, we don't object to criminals being eliminated. We don't object to terrorists being eliminated. But just in theory, you understand. If you were involved in removing some criminals from our midst, the government might be willing to offer you amnesty for any such actions, in return for you giving us your full cooperation in this case."

"Mind if I get some coffee?" Startled by the agent's words, Townsend made sure to keep his voice even.

"Go right ahead." Townsend walked into the kitchen and poured steaming black coffee into a mug. He took a sip and a deep breath. He body moved slowly but his mind was racing. After another glug of coffee, he returned to the living room and sat down again

"Come to a conclusion, Mr. Townsend?"

"I've been mulling over a few things." He swirled the coffee around in his cup. "A very interesting proposal. Let us say – in theory, of course…"

"Of course."

"…that your suggestion seems to have possibilities. But there is one option you might have overlooked. Sometimes things are not always as they seem. Would the amnesty still stand if a person could add only a minimal amount of information to your case?" Townsend asked.

The two CIA agents frowned as they looked at each other. "You wouldn't be lying to us, would you, Mr. Townsend?" Denton asked.

Townsend shook his head. "I am a rational man. In my business, I state my fee and do my job. There is no negotiation and no bargaining. If my client cannot pay my price or prefers to haggle, I exit. I do not play games. I would be a lousy poker player because I could not bluff well. I have reason to believe that the information I have would not help your case much. I can give you a name and some other data, which may prove useful, but it will not resolve your investigation. As an offer of my sincerity, I will tell you again that I have never seen the person you call 'The Badger'. He may have been behind the scenes, of course, but I never laid eyes on him."

"But there were other people whom you dealt with?"

"Yes, one person in particular. But there is a twist to this case — a surprise that made it a very easy assignment for me. It was the easiest money I ever made. But you will not be as pleased by the surprise as I was. I'm telling you this upfront so you won't feel cheated if we go ahead with the deal." The two looked at one another again. Both of them felt that Townsend was being honest with them.

"Do you have a room where we can consult privately?" Hadley said. Townsend pointed to a hallway. "Two doors down on your left is my study. Make yourself at home. Make a phone call if you like. There are no bugs in the room." Townsend waited patiently.

In about fifteen minutes, the two men returned and sat down on the sofa. "The deal is still on," Hadley said. "There is amnesty if you tell us everything you know about the

Wesley Hunter case. Minimal or major, you will be in the clear if you level with us."

"Gentleman, the Hunter case was not only the easiest I've ever had – it has become the luckiest case I've ever taken too."

Chapter 15

Summerlin, Nevada

The waitress, her blonde, curly hair flowing down behind her neck, squinted as she looked at the photo. She made a series of tics, hiccups and moans as she flipped the picture up and down. "Does he look familiar?" Sandi Burnside asked.

"Somewhat. I seem to remember him, vaguely. We see so many people here – the faces tend to merge together." She held the photograph in one hand and pointed to it with a finger on her other hand. "But I do seem to recall this guy. Yes, I think it was around the time we had that big storm. Six, eight inches of snow. I didn't think we'd get many customers that day." She tapped the image with her finger. "But this guy came in, very calm, wearing a little porkpie hat. Very courteous. Smiling a lot. I thought, he's the type to give a big tip. And he did. Ten dollars, if I remember, for two cups of coffee."

"Do you remember if he was sitting with anyone the day he came in?" Sandi asked.

"Yes. He was alone at a small table for a while. Just kept sipping his coffee and didn't seem to have a care in the world. Some people get upset and fidgety when they're waiting for someone. But not him. He just drank his coffee and seemed perfectly content. I asked him if he wanted anything else and he said very pleasantly that no, he would just wait. It must have been fifteen or twenty minutes until his friend joined him. Maybe he'd got held up by the snow."

"Did you know who the friend was?"

The girl shook her head. "No, I didn't recognize him. He was bundled up, but he was a younger man. Pale, with sideburns. And the thing is, he looked like a bundle of nerves next to this guy. The younger man was agitated, edgy, always looking around. I thought he was going to order a decaf but he had something else."

"Did you happen to overhear any of their conversation?"

"No. When I wasn't taking their order I stayed away. Just took the order of the younger guy, brought it back and then asked the older gentleman if he wanted anything else. He didn't."

"The young guy's name? Did he mention it?"

The waitress bit her lower lip. "No. The only reason I remember him is because I was thinking the older guy would be a great tipper, which he was. But the young guy was stingy as Scrooge. If he left anything at all it was just a couple of quarters. That's why I remembered him. He was with the eco-group. Protecting the poor and the oppressed, apparently. When it came to tipping, he wasn't exactly helping the poor. Not by a long shot."

"His name?"

She bit her lip again. "No, I don't think I heard it. But he stayed until the older man had gone. I did recognize his second friend, who came in about five minutes after the other guy left."

"Who was his second friend?"

"Steven Gifford. Works for the oil company. He comes in here often."

"Gifford? Did you say Steven Gifford?"

"Yes, he's a very nice man. You can ask him who his friend was."

"I'll be sure to do that." Sandi grasped a fifty-dollar bill and handed it over. "Thank you very much." She looked at the picture. So Mr. Gifford has a friend who knew Mr. Townsend. Were all of them friends? she wondered.

Chapter 16

Elm Grove, Nevada

Six Months Later

Sandi looked again at the black and white sketch after she'd driven into the parking lot of the Hunter Oil Company headquarters in Elm Grove. A friend of hers was a pretty good artist and the woman had done a good job on the little information Sandi had provided. She'd grilled the waitresses on what the mysterious stranger at the coffee shop looked like and her artist friend had drawn what Sandi thought was a very good composite. She gently folded the sketch once and put it into her purse. Then she walked briskly into the office and told the secretary she was here to see Steven Gifford. He was waiting for her, the secretary said. Gifford rose from his desk and offered his hand when she walked into his office. "Sandi, hello. It's been a while since I've seen you," he said.

"Steven. It has been a while."

"I meant to offer my condolences at the funeral but you seemed too busy. Every time I wanted to come over, you seemed to have three people around you." He waved his hand for her to sit down.

She sat. "I understand. But there's something I need to ask you about."

Back behind his desk, Steven nodded. "What can I do for you?"

She reached into her purse and pulled out the sketch. Unfolding it, she handed it to Gifford. "Can you tell me if you know this man? The drawing may not be 100 percent accurate but I hope it's a reasonable facsimile of the man." Gifford studied the photo.

To Sandi, the executive looked slightly annoyed. His fingers clasped his chin and covered his mouth. "It bears a resemblance to Thomas Valdane," he said.

"Who's he?"

"A local student, I believe. To be honest, I'm not sure he has a job. But he is also a so-called environmental activist. Dr. Bill told me that he'd just had a meeting with three such activists, one being Thomas Valdane. He's bothered about fossil fuels, and has all the pseudo-arguments against it.

"Have you ever seen him outside of such official meetings?"

Gifford narrowed his eyes and stared again at the portrait. "I don't think so. Oil people and anti-fossil fuel activists rarely hang out together. Why do you ask?" He handed back the picture.

Sandi leaned back in the chair and crossed her legs. She couldn't discern whether Gifford was lying or not. But even though she knew that her father trusted the man, suspicions were growing with her. "Steven, two days after my father died, a professional killer was spotted in Elm Grove. He was walking in one of our city parks with another man who has not yet been identified. The professional is a man named Oliver Townsend. He's a middle-age guy who looks like he could play Santa Claus at Christmas, but he is a killer."

Gifford nodded. "How do you know this?"

"That's irrelevant right now. Besides, I'm a reporter – I don't reveal my sources. Suffice to say that Mr. Townsend used our local Starbucks. His credit card was used to pay a bill there. While relaxing and drinking coffee, he met a second man." She held up the drawing. "This man."

Gifford's voice was wary. "How can you be sure of that?"

"I am. The 'how' is again irrelevant. What is more important is that after the meeting with Townsend, another gentleman came and spoke with Valdane." Her eyes narrowed. "You did, Steven."

"I did?" She nodded. "According to several witnesses. They know you at Starbucks. You're a regular customer and you tip well."

"May I see that portrait again?" She handed it to him.

He studied it for a minute. Sandi wondered if he was pondering telling the truth or concocting a plausible lie. He sighed and handed the picture back. "When did this happen?"

"Two days before my father died."

"I don't remember all of my trips to Starbucks. As you noted, I am a regular customer there. But now that you mention it, I do remember rushing in one day about two weeks ago and seeing Valdane there. He asked me to join him and I think I did spend a few minutes chatting with him."

"What were you talking about?"

Gifford shrugged. "Same things we always talk about – oil and the environment. They're the only things are on Valdane's mind. He is singularly focused."

"And you just went over to say hello?"

"It's important in this business to be civil and courteous even to our opponents. I saw no harm in going to his table and chatting for a few minutes. I had no idea he'd just been talking to a hit-man. I…I can't picture him doing anything violent. Valdane's always seemed dedicated and passionate. A bit analytical about his beliefs, perhaps, but not violent."

"Sometimes fanatics can become so

"True, but Valdane…" He shrugged. "I guess you never really know, do you?"

"No," Sandi said, very slowly. "I guess you don't. Do you know where I can find Mr. Valdane?"

"Not really. We're not friends, so I don't have his address or phone number. But I do know he's affiliated with the Friends of the Earth group in town. I'm sure they'd know where to contact him."

"Thank you."

Gifford edged forwards and put his elbows on his desk. "Sandi, your father died due to a fall. Surely you don't think I had anything to do with his death? That would be absurd."

Sandi gave a quick smile. "Let's just say I'm asking questions. Mr. Townsend's presence in Elm Grove does give one pause for thought, doesn't it?"

"I guess you could say that." As Sandi walked back to her car, she felt a man's eyes focused on her. He watched her closely as she opened the door and climbed in, and frowned as she drove off. He blew out some air, then his teeth bit down on his lower lip, almost puncturing the skin.

He was not happy.

Chapter 17

The office of Friends of the Earth was a cozy residence full of environmental posters, ordinary furniture and students milling around. A green poster showing a smiling polar bear took up a quarter of the wall. The secretary looked efficient, but behind her smile of teeth and braces, there remained a suspicious look. Sandi realized, that compared to the students, she looked very 'establishment'. Rich and establishment. Even so, she inquired about Thomas Valdane.

"Yes, he is one of our officers but I'm afraid he's busy now. I was told that he won't be able to see anybody until tomorrow."

Sandi gave her a patronizing smile. "Oh, that's a shame, dear. I'm a reporter from the local television station and I just wanted to ask Mr. Valdane about why environmental monies slated for this group are being transferred to terrorist organizations. But I can do the story without a comment from him." Ten seconds later, when she was escorted into Valdane's office, he was not amused. He said nothing, but merely glared at her with an angry frown as she walked in and sat down.

"I didn't find that funny, Ms....what was your name again?" Vadane said.

"Sandi Burnside."

"Oh, yes. I've seen you on the air. I thought you were a good reporter, until now."

"I'm not interested in what you think of my journalistic skills. I want to know why you met with Oliver Townsend."

"Who? I don't know any Oliver Townsend."

"I'll show you a picture of him. It's possible that he didn't use his real name when he dealt with you." She lifted the photo of Townsend from her purse and sailed it onto the desk. When Valdane picked it up, he flinched with recognition.

"So you do know him," Sandi said.

"I never said that. He's an average-looking man." But Valdane's voice was weak, faulty. He shook his head and coughed before his voice came back. "I...I don't..."

"Cut the crap, Mr. Valdane. You were seen with this man, who happens to be a professional killer and, I'm told, is very good at his work. Whom did you want killed?"

Valdane tried to answer but the weak syllables fell to the floor. He coughed again, then managed a "I don't know what you're talking about, Ms. Burnside. I may have bumped into this man...I can't say. I see a lot of people."

"You're full of it. You had coffee with this man. Did you discuss the latest assassination techniques? You were at the local Starbucks. Waitresses can identify you. For all your rhetoric about helping the poor and saving the Earth, you are a lousy tipper. Waitresses remember things like that. They know the generous customers from the cheapskates."

His cheeks reddened. "I didn't have any extra money that day. I…"

"So you were there with Townsend?" Valdane was silent for a moment.

"I've seen the man around campus. I don't know what he was doing there."

"Starbucks isn't located on campus. It's downtown."

Valdane looked at the picture again. "I might have seen him…"

"On his credit card were charges for two coffees. He was paying that day - he bought your coffee. Now you can answer my question or you can answer to the FBI. Which will it be?"

He kicked the desk and slammed his chair back into the wall. He spat the words out. "You rich people think you know everything, don't you?"

"Yes, because we generally do." Sandi's voice was uncharacteristically sharp . "I didn't come here to discuss wealth. Why were you talking to a killer?"

"I didn't know he was a killer. I'd seen him around. Said his name was Smith. I was at Starbucks some time ago and he invited me to his table. So I sat down. He'd come by the office a day or so before."

"This office?" Sandi asked. Valdane nodded.

"Why would he do that?"

"To give us a contribution. He said he admired our work and wanted to help the cause. I happened to be out in the lobby when he came by. So I thanked him and we chatted for a few minutes. He didn't tell me his business and I didn't ask. I certainly didn't realize he was a hit-man. If, in fact, he is."

"Oh, he is. It's a fact."

"I had no knowledge of that."

"You're a liar, Mr. Valdane and not a very good one. "We'll see about that." Sandi said as she stood up. She continued to glare at the man behind the desk. "I never trust a bad tipper."

"Get out! Valdane's voice was rising. I don't have to sit and listen to this. I happened to visit and chat with a contributor to our valuable work when he spotted me at Starbucks recently. That's all. What he does for a living is something I have no knowledge of. Don't come back!"

Steaming, Sandi stood up and walked out of his office. What a horrible little man, she uttered under her breath.

Chapter 18

Elm Grove, Nevada

Seven Months Later

Harry Burnside's hard, dark eyes stared at FBI Agent Upton. He stood up then sat down and slowly whirled back around in the black swivel office chair, arcing in a semi-circle. The stony frown was frozen on his face. The tip of an incisor showed over a lower lip. "You've got to be kidding me, Brad, and this is not a subject to joke about."

The FBI agent shook his head and took a seat opposite Harry. "I know it sounds a bit fantastical, but that's the story we've got and what little evidence we have corroborates the story."

Harry swirled again in the chair. "So you're telling me that when Oliver Townsend, noted hit-man, went to this very house to kill Dr. Wes Hunter, he found the doctor already dead?"

"That's what we have."

"And the FBI is buying that?"

"For now, yes." Harry nodded. "Townsend had no reason to lie. He was offered amnesty for his crimes. Even if he had killed the doctor, it would have been overlooked. He told us he was hired by a man named Thomas Valdane. He believed the name was fake. Gave us a description of the man but said that he suspected Valdane wore make-up, fake hair, fake sideburns, etc., so not to expect him to match the description."

"Did the man say why he wanted Dr. Wes dead?"

"Not in so many words. It was clear he disliked the doctor but he never specified the reason, and Townsend never asked. He doesn't much care for his clients' reasons. Apparently the man did say once that, "It was time the past caught up with Dr. Hunter.""

Harry scratched his chin. "The past eventually catches up with all of us. What was in Dr. Wes's past that caught up with him? Of course, it could have been a imagined slight or even something honorable that some malignant thug objected to."

"It doesn't exactly narrow down the field, but the suspects are few. Think we can rule out any international connections," Upton added. "The mysterious terrorist?"

"Yes." Upton shifted in his chair. "It was a theory for a while. A few more intelligent and cunning terrorists see the possibilities in shale oil, and frightening possibilities open up. Obviously they'd like the Middle East to keep its stranglehold on oil, because they hope to one day control the Middle East. If we stop needing Middle East oil and start selling to their customers instead of buying, then that region of the world becomes insignificant. When there was a rumor that 'The Badger' had surfaced, we thought perhaps the terrorists might use murder and sabotage to cripple shale oil production. A bit far-fetched, perhaps, but history has shown that conspiracy theorists are insufficiently pessimistic."

Harry laughed. "I'll have to write that down. Would you like a drink, Brad?"

"As a matter of fact, yes. Got any bourbon?"

"I have the best bourbon there is." Harry walked to the bar, dropped ice cubes into two glasses and poured the bourbon in. He took one glass and handed it to his friend. Upton took a long gulp. He sighed and smiled as he held up the glass.

"You weren't kidding. That's excellent."

As Harry moved back behind his desk, Upton leaned forward, balancing his elbows on his knees. He swirled the liquor around in his glass. "Were you aware of the...serious disagreement that Dr. Wes had with a fellow physician at the hospital?"

"The sexual harassment charge?"

"That one."

"Heard about that. Haven't looked into it yet, though."

"Apparently, a long-term friendship has been destroyed. That can lead to bad things. But after Townsend told us what his client said, we're focusing on Dr. Wes's past, not recent events."

Harry sipped from his glass. "So are you thinking Dr. Wes's death was not from natural causes?"

"We're reconsidering everything and have exhumed Dr. Hunter's body for additional tests. Perhaps the local examiner overlooked something. The case appeared to be cut and dried. But maybe we assumed facts that were not in evidence. That bump on the head, for instance, may not have caused his death."

"But it might have triggered something in his brain. He was having migraines, and they were possibly a symptom of something more serious," said Harry. "I've talked to Dr. Ross. I know he had some concerns so we want a more detailed examination."

"Can't hurt, I guess." Upton leaned back in his seat and drained his glass. "Mind if I have another?" he asked Harry.

"Help yourself."

Upton walked to the bar and poured more bourbon into his glass. "There's something else you might like to know. I could save you some investigative time."

"You don't have too. I'm billed by the hour and I get paid well," replied Harry.

"You can still bill for the information – you just don't have to work for it," Upton laughed.

"That's every private detective's dream. Every lawyer's dream too," Harry said.

Upton returned to his seat and said, "The housekeeper. Marian Hinkley."

"What about her?" asked Harry.

"That's not her real name. She was born Evelyn Madigan fifty-some years ago. She's also a natural blonde. Upton paused and continued. "How many women change their hair color to brown from blonde instead of the other way around?"

"Maybe a long-ago boyfriend preferred brunettes" Harry replied.

"Or maybe she wanted to hide something."

"Been checking her background?"

"We're checking everyone's background, including yours. We had thought Dr. Hunter's death and the sabotage up in Idaho might have international connections, so we checked everybody." Upton smiled. "You're a member of some subversive groups, Harry."

The private detective laughed. "Only anti-tax groups. I don't believe in taxes."

"Who does? Anyway, she became Marian Hinkley about ten years ago. She had given up Evelyn Madigan a long time ago, possible in college. She likes to change her name."

"A harmless hobby."

"She grew up in LA, left briefly while she was young and then came back and had a child there. Now he's with the Hunter Oil Company. Works here as an executive/engineer. She had a variety of jobs before coming to work for Dr. Hunter, but never as a housekeeper."

"You can have different careers and different names. Variety is the spice of life."

"How true," Upton said, swallowing his second drink. "Do any other investigation of the family? About, say Dr. Ross and Maggie Hunter?"

"Well, they were often out of the country at the same time and were often seen in Paris at the same time. But I don't want to draw conclusions."

"Damn, you did do some investigating."

"The international angle bothered us until we ruled it out. Can't be too cautious nowadays."

"You obviously aren't," Harry said.

"Well, we like to think the taxpayers are not wasting their money on our salaries."

"So have you ruled the couple out as suspects or are they still on your list?" asked Harry

"Well, Maggie wasn't here at the time of the murder, although she could have hired someone. Or they, as a couple, could have hired someone. But I tend to rule them out. To be honest, a lot of wives cheat on their husbands without killing them. I tend to doubt Dr. Ross is a killer, or would even employ a hired hit-man. Sleeping with the woman you love, even if she's married to another man, is very different to murder." Upton concluded.

"And there you have it," Harry said.

Chapter 19

Sandi Burnside appreciated that her boss was allowing her to pursue her investigation solely, without worrying about other news. She was at her computer at the television station. Although there was a TV monitor on, the volume was turned so low that it might as well have been mute. A tall brunette stood up, reporting on the city council (at least, the city hall was in the background), but Sandi paid little attention to her. She pressed keys on her computer. It's amazing the amount of information you can get in the Internet nowadays, she thought. Almost everything. There's little privacy left in the world. Soon privacy will be a thing of the past.

Even so, there was very little information on Thomas Valdane that she could uncover. It's possible that the name was phony, she thought. The odds were against it, though. More probable was that Valdane had done very little to be recorded. He had been born 25 years ago in Riverside, California and was educated in the Riverdale schools. He had no police record and, although grades are supposed to be confidential, Sandi learned that he was an honor student. He seemed to have taken several years off after high school and gradually moved into the environmental movement, participating in several demonstrations in Seattle and

Portland against big oil companies. The protests were loud but not violent. He wound up in Elm Grove and attended Landmont College, located about ten miles outside the city limits. Landmont was a small but well-respected college, which had a particularly distinguished reputation in the sciences, including environmental science.

Valdane had quickly become vice president of the regional Friends of the Earth organization, definitely an anti-fossil fuel group but one that had eschewed violence. "So why," asked Sandi aloud, "would he be talking with a hired killer? They'd hardly just be discussing the special blends of coffee." Still, Valdane had lied to her, at least at first. And he'd definitely looked uncomfortable when she'd mentioned Townsend. She would bet big money that the little meeting at Starbucks hadn't been an accident. Valdane knew who Townsend was and what he did for a living. On Valdane's Facebook page, there were several pictures of him. He had not written anything on it for a week. It listed him as the VP of the Friends of the Earth chapter, a student at Landmont and an environmental activist. In one, he posed with three other people in front of the FOE office. His friends list was innocuous, except for one man with dark hair and dark, bushy eyebrows. The black hair contrasted with the pale, round face, with lips and nose that were both too big. The man looked menacing. His name was Lester Riley, but his Facebook page revealed nothing. He had not used it for months.

She rolled back in her chair but stared at the screen. She checked the Friends of the Earth page but it revealed nothing of interest. Detective work = ninety-nine percent legwork, she thought. Or nowadays, fifty-five percent computer work, forty-four percent legwork. She hit the correct button on her office phone and punched in her ex-husband's number. His booming voice came on the line in ten seconds. "Harry, this is the ex-wife you pine for."

"How true. Want to get married again?"

For a moment she was silent. A dull sense of apprehension seemed to be clouding her brain. "You know today I am especially pensive. Full of melancholy and regret. Don't ask that again or I might say yes."

"Fine with me, honey. I've been having a few regrets lately too." Harry replied self-confidently.

Uppermost in her thoughts were the events of the day. Sandi shook herself. For a minute she thought of pursuing the conversation. The two had clashed in their marriage but, all in all, they had made a good couple. However, there were other, more pressing matters. "Let's discuss that later. I wanted to tell you about my little session at the Friends of the Earth club."

Sandi related her meeting with Valdane and her session with Gifford. Harry listened carefully. When she'd finished, Harry told her about his conversation with FBI Agent Upton. "So what do you think?" Sandi asked

"You go first."

"Well, I think Valdane lied to me at first. Then he denied knowing anything about Townsend but I'm guessing he knew his coffee partner was a hit-man." Sandi added.

"Does seem like it."

"Think you could ask your FBI friend to squeeze a little more information out of Townsend? Let him tell us what his conversation with Valdane was about?"

129

"I thought my favor share was exhausted with the FBI but I'll see if I can pull one more out of the hat." Harry replied. "The FBI asked Townsend about his assignment and he gave them Valdane but they didn't go any further with the questioning. They should have."

"Besides, if I had known the FBI had closed on Townsend, I would have mentioned that to Valdane." Sandi said. "That would have made him sweat, knowing Townsend was singing to the FBI. Maybe I should go back."

"No, let me get the information from Townsend through the bureau. Perhaps they were discussing coffee imports, but let's make sure. So what do you make of the information on our housekeeper?"

Sandi laughed. "A lot of people change their names." She shrugged. "But I wonder what she would look like as a blonde." Sandi remembered looking at her dad's college album and there were many blondes in those pictures. She promised to revisit those photos soon.

"So would you like dinner? I'll buy." Harry said.

"What a wonderful offer. Let's go to Cavello's. The best steaks in town."

"Yes, the best steaks in the city. The best steaks in the region, for that matter," Harry said. "See you there in thirty minutes."

"Okay. It's a date."

Chapter 20

Ten minutes later, Sandi walked out of the office. The television station building was isolated and set back into the tall forests just east of the city. The parking lot was in the front of the building. She reached for the door as she heard the roaring engine of a car speeding past. Later, she thought, she may have subconsciously picked something up. Some antediluvian instinct had sent fiery warnings from her brain to her spine. She ducked as the two bullets whizzed over her head.

In high school and at college, she had competed in athletics and she still exercised regularly. So when she hit the hard asphalt, she rolled instead of grasping in pain, as the rough gravel cut into her skin. She heard a third bullet plunk into the concrete two inches to her left. The car roared off and she rolled under a truck. She watched the mysterious assailant speed into the street and down the highway. She crawled out from under the dirty engine and brushed herself off. Her shoulder was aching and a few thin lines of blood snaked down her arms. "Just another routine day at the office," she said aloud, still glaring at the road.

By the time she entered the restaurant and set down at the table, she'd bandaged the scrapes and washed the grime off her face. She ordered a double Martini when the waitress approached, surprising her ex-husband. "I've had a tough day," she said. "When I get the drink I'll give you specifics."

Harry watched her closely and noticed that she was shaken but not stirred. He ordered a bourbon, but watched as Sandi took the first sip from her scotch. Then she told him about the attempt on her life. "Sandi, we should go to the police," Harry said.

She shook her head. "The police, the FBI and a few other federal agencies from what I can tell are already involved. I'd thought we'd talk this over. But from now on I'm carrying my Beretta."

"Still practising?"

"Yes. I've gotten pretty good at the range. Maybe I will get a chance to see how good I am with a moving target." Harry smiled. He wasn't surprised that Sandi took a murder attempt with such nonchalance. She was a tough lady. The two paused for a moment while a waitress came. They ordered steaks and Sandi asked for a second drink. She'd already drained her glass. When the waitress left, she edged closer to Harry. "In my previous years of reporting, I've had a few threats – I think every reporter has experienced that – but until now, no one has actually taken a shot at me. So logically, I'm thinking that the attempt must be connected to my most recent investigation."

"Sounds reasonable."

"If that's true, then my father did not die of natural causes, and somebody wants to keep the real cause of his death a secret."

"Logical. And we take that one more step…"

"Then we could say that the attack came after I confronted Steven Gifford and Thomas Valdane," Sandi said, taking a swig from her second drink.

Harry nodded, but raised a finger. "That's circumstantial. There is no direct connection between the two events, although there is suspicion. Someone might have been tailing you all day." Sandi shook as if mildly slapped. She edged back in her chair.

"True. I didn't think of that. I might have attracted someone's attention before going into the oil office. But I didn't notice anyone."

"Doubtful you would have done. You were focused on one thing – the investigation. I doubt you would have noticed anyone following you."

"No, but I will now, if it happens again."

"What information did you pick up from Gifford and Valdane?"

Sandi recounted their conversations. "I think Gifford was a bit taken aback. After all, it does appear odd to be talking to a hit-man – or even to a second man who was talking to a hit man – but it could have been innocent. Valdane was definitely edgy and nervous. He was acting like a criminal."

"You had an interesting day and I will make it even more interesting. I had a meeting with Mr. Upton earlier." Sandi listened intently as Harry related the conversation. "The FBI thinks it's ruled out any international connections. They're talking with Mr. Townsend and have discovered that Marian Hinkley, or whatever her name is, is a natural blonde. They do good work."

"When they go into high gear, they can be amazing. Get a bad agent now and then but most of them are first-rate," Sandi said. "But Townsend never said why his client wanted Dad dead?"

"No, but Townsend didn't ask. A hit-man doesn't care about the reasons; he just carries out the job. Townsend did say that his client said Dr. Wes deserved it."

"But if the FBI is correct, we can eliminate any overseas operation," said Sandi.

"Yes, that brings it closer to home. There was an incident of sabotage up in Idaho not too long ago. An arson at the Hunter Oil fields. The FBI suspects radical environmentalists, but Upton seemed to doubt they would stoop to murder." The two sat for a while without talking. The waitress brought their steaks. They were halfway through the meal before Harry spoke again. "There's something I should tell you that you may not know. Came across it during my investigation."

At first, Sandi was shocked and denied it. "That doesn't sound like, Dad."

"He was a young man who had a fling. He never knew that you and Bill have a half-brother somewhere."

Sandi ate the rest of her steak in silence. She ate the slice of apple pie ordered as dessert also without saying a word. But her mind was working, thinking, putting together all the random threads. Even though Harry was her ex-husband, she still knew how his mind worked.

As the waitress took away the plates, Sandi looked at her former husband. "Are you wondering the same thing I am?"

"You know me well. I think I am." She reached over and clasped his hand.

"From time to time, Harry, I regret we split up." He patted her hand. "I feel the same way. But first things first."

"If we're thinking the same thing, do you have the same idea I do?"

He nodded. "Probably."

"Think it would work?"

"I'd say there's an eight in ten chance. Odds are pretty good."

"We can lay the groundwork tomorrow. I'm going home now."

Chapter 21

Nine Months Later

The FBI agent, Brad Upton, gave one final courtesy call to his colleague, Harry Burnside, to let him know of the autopsy results for Dr. Wes Hunter. The pathologists's conclusion had not surprised him in the slightest.

"So it was murder, and he didn't die from falling down the stairs?" Harry said.

"Whoever did it intended to kill the doctor in a way that wouldn't leave a trace. I wonder if…never mind."

"It would appear so. And did you remember the other item I asked you about?"

"Stanford," Upton said. "That's where Dr. Wes went to college. They have a very good medical program there."

"I know."

"I think that seals it," Harry said.

"No real evidence yet. But I'm working on it."

"So am I."

Chapter 22

Marian Hinkley was apprehensive when she learned that the authorities were exhuming the body of Dr. Wes Hunter. Why shouldn't they let the man rest in peace? Things had moved too fast. She needed a vacation and planned to take one. Her suitcase was opened on her bed and she hastily folded her clothes and placed them neatly inside. Her car was three years old but in good condition. It had only 55,000 miles on it, hardly broken in. I had very good gas mileage on the highway. And she was going on the highway, or the Interstate to be more precise. Elm Grove had not been kind to her. She wanted the place in her rear-view mirror as soon as possible.

The overnight bag had already been packed. It lay beside her bed. She looked anxiously toward the door. The large Hunter mansion provided a spacious residence for the housekeeper. There was not only a bedroom but a small dining room and a living space where there was sofa and chairs. She walked briskly to the living room with her suitcase, then was startled by a voice.

"Going somewhere, Marian?" She dropped the suitcase and looked around. Sandi Burnside leaned against the wall. She had an odd smile on her face. Marian stuttered out a reply.

"Ye...s, ma'am? This is all getting too much for me. The death of Dr. Wes...and everything else. I just wanted to get away for a while...with your permission, of course. I was going to ask you later but I was sure you wouldn't mind."

If possible, Sandi's odd smile became even stranger. But she spoke with a condescending tone. "Oh, I guess I don't mind, Marian. But perhaps the FBI might."

"Ma'am, why would you say that?" asked Marian.

Sandi walked a few steps into the room. "I suppose you got upset when you heard about the exhumation of Dad's body. A federal pathologist was brought in, you know? The regular pathologist we have here is good, but the federal man is trained in poisons and toxicology."

"I don't follow you," Marian said, a note of worry coming into her voice.

"The autopsy showed poison in Dad's system. Slow-acting poison that would take a while to take effect. It was administered over a period of time. Almost untraceable. Almost. So I imagine the FBI will be asking who could have given Dad the poison over a period of time. Possibly the housekeeper who prepared his meals? She'd be the obvious suspect, wouldn't you agree?" Marian said nothing.

Her dark eyes darted their gaze around the room. She slumped down in a chair. But her hand reached down to the suitcase and flipped it open. "I don't know what to say. I didn't poison Dr. Wes. He fell."

"But that wasn't what killed him. Even at his age, Dad was a strong man. It took a lot more poison than you thought to finish him off, didn't it? He must have been getting weaker but had such a strong will that he pushed his body, so no one realized what was happening. He had that darned Type-A personality. So he never slowed down, even when the poison was killing him."

"I don't know what you're talking about," Marian said dismissively.

"But he was weak that night, wasn't he? I'm guessing he staggered from the study and slipped on the stairs. Or he could have been pushed, of course. Marian? Did you push him?"

Marian shook her head. "I understand your grief, but you are making outrageous allegations."

"And I think we both know why. Because of that long-ago incident. But it wasn't Dad's fault. It was you who never told him about the child."

Marian whipped the knife from the suitcase. Shocked, Sandi took two steps back. "But I did!" Marian spat the words out. The malice colored her voice. "That night I told him. I wanted Steven to have an inheritance. He deserved it. But Wes rejected it. He said he didn't believe me."

"The poison had probably affected his mind. He was dying. Dad was generous. Anyway, it doesn't matter now."

Marian raised the knife and strode toward Sandi. "Why should you enjoy the benefits of your father's wealth when my son can't? Steven knew, but he wanted nothing to do with the Hunter family. Yet he deserved to have a share. Your father didn't even recognize me."

"It was a long time ago, Marian."

"It was yesterday!" she yelled.

Sandi edged back another step but strong hands suddenly locked on her arms. Her head bumped against someone's chest. She struggled but the man held her tight.

"Thomas, I was expecting you," Marian said.

"Two Hunters can be killed now, instead of one. So much the better. You were destroying the Earth, just the way your father destroyed Marian," said Valdane.

"Were you involved too?" Sandi asked.

"No, he wasn't!" Marian snarled. "But he knew of it. He hated your father as much as I did. He was friends with my son, even though they are on opposite sides of the environmental fence. Steven is friends with everyone. He likes everyone. There's not a malicious bone in his body."

"Didn't get much genetic heritage from his mother, did he?" Sandi said. She struggled but Valdane held her tight.

"You were the one who shot at me," she said looking around at Valdane.

"Yes. Alas, I missed. But Marian won't." Valdane spat out the words.

Marian edged closer to her. "Poison is better. I hate to kill with a knife. It's messy and bloody. But I have no choice."

She raised the knife, but yelled in agony as the bullet crashed into her hand. The knife fell to the floor. A second bullet creased Valdane's skull. He groaned and spun into a wall, then dropped.

"Harry, what took you so long?" Sandi screamed.

"We wanted to get a confession, didn't we?" he replied. Marian groaned again and held up her hand. Blood ran across her fingers and dropped on the carpet. Harry handed her a handkerchief.

"Call 911," he said.

Sandi already had her phone in her hand. "You know, Harry, I'm so glad you stopped by. I don't know how I ever let you get away. Her head began to throb. Sandi placed her hands over her ears to shut out the ambulance and police sirens. She walked slowly towards Harry, "Darling, how did you…"

Harry reached into his coat pocket, pulled out the old college picture and pointed to the blonde behind Dr. Wes. "I wanted you to see this."

"Anyone who would stoop to using poison isn't going to have guts enough to use a gun or a knife." Sandi said looking over at Marian.

The sirens got louder as police vehicles and an ambulance screeched to a halt in the driveway. Three policemen and a detective rushed into the house with their weapons drawn. "Put your hands up and drop your weapons!" they shouted in unison. They noticed that the older woman was alive, blood on her arm and dripping from her fingers. A man lay face down at the other end of the room. One of the policemen rushed towards Valdane and checked for any signs of life. "This man is dead," he said.

"Marian Hinkley?" The police detective read the housekeeper her rights. "Come with us."

Sandi's eyes were moist as she stared across as Marian. "How could you be so cruel to my family?"

"I never meant to hurt you," Marian began in a slow, measured tone. "I only wanted Wes to acknowledge that

143

Steven, my Steven, was our son and his heir…" Marian's voice trailed off.

"Come now, Mrs. Hinkley," said the police detective. "You'll have your day in court."

The detective turned to Harry and Sandi. "Would you both care to make a statement at the station? Or right here?"

"We'll do it here," said Sandi nodding in Harry's direction. "If that's okay?"

The detective had no objection to their request. He left an hour later with the most recent information that Harry and Sandi had gathered, promising to return in a day or two for the remaining evidence.

Harry placed an arm around Sandi's shoulder. "I know I behaved badly. But we can re-arrange things. Sandi, I want to have another chance at our happiness."

Leaning her head against his shoulder. "Well," she began, "I'll have to think about it."

"Ssshh," Harry said softly, placing one finger on her lips and kneeling down in front of her. "You don't have to answer now. We've already met. Only this time…this time, it depends on whether you believe in happy endings."

Made in the USA
Middletown, DE
29 June 2019